## Everyone in town liked Barney— *almost* everyone...

At least it seemed that way until he was found shot to death in a field just outside of town. The police said it was a hunting accident.

But Felix Oberstdorf didn't think it was an accident. He was a good friend of Barney's. He insisted that it was murder and he started to investigate. And he continued, even though his own life was clearly in danger.

He found out a lot—enough to blow the lid off the sleepy little town of Hessberg.

# A PLACE LIKE HESSBERG

**Charles Fleet**

A RAVEN HOUSE MYSTERY FROM
# W🌐RLDWIDE
TORONTO • LONDON • NEW YORK • SYDNEY

Raven House edition published January 1982

Second printing January 1982

ISBN 0-373-63017-4

1

WHENEVER ANYBODY DIES in a place like Hessberg, everybody knows about it and a lot of people go to the funeral. And, like as not, the event gets a column on the first page of the weekly newspaper, and the county welfare department usually gets involved, because in most cases the person is elderly and has been drawing old age assistance. If not that, then the departed may have been a state hospital patient buried at county expense. This is especially true of Hessberg, which happens to be the location of Midwest State Hospital, formerly the Hessberg Insane Asylum. The reason that it was changed to Midwest State Hospital is that we are located about halfway across the state, from east to west. When it was decided, a quarter century ago, that *insane asylum* was neither an accurate nor a dignified term, the change was made. That was not the only change made. With the advent of widespread drug therapy, the population of the institution began to decline steadily. The only coal mine in our part of the state began to peter out about the same time, resulting in a severe blow to our economy. Closing of the mine cost fifty jobs at once, and over a period of time, the dwindling numbers at Midwest resulted in another fifty job losses. That is a big loss to a small town, and our economy has been shaky for a long time, although we are a county-seat town in a rich agricultural district.

True, it is still a good place to live. We get the same television shows that people get anywhere else, the same brands of beer and gasoline, and at the same time, enjoy the relaxation of a rural environment. We are only two hours by highway from Winnebago City and three hours from Omaha. We managed to increase our population slightly in the last census period, bringing us up to eleven hundred and fourteen. Besides the hospital, which still provides employment for a hundred and fifty, the courthouse harbors a hundred, and then there are the Braunholz elevators and the Emhoff Feedlot Company. Between them, these enterprises employ another eighty-five. So, we may be lucky at that, in terms of industry and employment.

We are right on the junction of State Highway 87 and Interstate 90, as well as on the main line of the Blue Hills and Prairie Railroad, and we get a fair amount of tourist trade. This makes it possible for our family to make three or four thousand dollars selling antiques during the summer months. My wife runs a little shop on Colfax Avenue, the main drag of Hessberg. She gets a pretty good play from vacationers zipping back and forth between the Blue Hills and points east. Without that, we couldn't make it on my salary as county welfare director. For although it is geographically a large county, we don't have many people to pay taxes in Kornfeld County. The farms and ranches are large, the population sparse, and like a lot of farmers and ranchers, those in our county are not overly religious about paying taxes. You try to pin one of the biggies down on his income, and he will probably come up with a figure like five or six thousand. He neglects to count the milk and eggs that he and his family consume, and the meat that he butchers, much less the fuel that he buys for his tractors and burns in his Mercedes Benz or Cadillac, with a subsequent saving in taxes. He counts his net income after all expenses, including improvement on his buildings and fences, new machinery, and Caribbean cruises, which are construed as business trips. Really we are a rich county, but a poor county, if you follow me. We bury our dead for two hundred dollars, including the casket, if it's a county funeral. That's why most of the sun-drenched, weedy graves at the edge of our town cemetery are the graves of former welfare recipients. This does not include Barney Heffner, who did not happen to be on welfare. Old Barney was buried higher on the hill, looking out over the wide Deerhorn Valley. His services were at the Bethel Lutheran Church, Missouri Synod, and most of the Lutherans in Hessberg showed up, either at the church or at the cemetery. Like all the towns in Kornfeld County, Hessberg is about ninety percent German, and evenly divided between Lutherans and Catholics, who hate each other's guts. You might suppose that in the early days a town would have been settled by people from the same place in Germany, and that they would have all been Catholic or all Lutheran, but it didn't happen that way. You show me a German community anywhere in the central west, and I'll show you a place that has a Catholic church and a Lutheran church. In these towns and villages, the feud between the Hatfields and the McCoys, or between the Capulets and the Montagues, would be a love feast.

In Hessberg, all the Lutheran matrons know exactly how many Catholic girls got pregnant and had to quit school during the year. At the same time, any Catholic housewife can tell you just which Lutheran girls are skinny-dipping at Blum's Lake, or fooling around with married men. It's uncanny, but that's how it is. If you have never lived in a Hessberg, you won't believe it. If you have lived in a Hessberg, you don't pay any attention to it, because that's just how it is.

When a person like Barney, who has lived in Hessberg all his life, turns up dead, people go into shock momentarily because everybody knows the person who is related to half the people in the county. There is a lot of wailing and moaning, and lip service to the Great White Voodoo Chief in the Temple. Many people offer sympathy and a few offer money, usually in a self-conscious, awkward manner. A few days after the funeral, people begin to think of the corpse as something in the distant past.

That was how it was with Barney, with one exception—me. Naturally his wife and kids continued to mourn, and maybe his brother in California. Chances are that his sister, Brenda Hoffman, bogged down in children and a perennial case of postpartum psychosis, suffered the loss for a long time. Otherwise, it was soon forgotten by all except me, Felix Oberstdorf, the fat little welfare director. Knowing Barney as I did, there was no question in my mind about his death. From the very beginning I knew that he had not died accidentally, that he had been murdered. For, having hunted with him, I knew that he was an expert who would never shoot himself in the belly while crawling over a fence. He was always the one to warn me: ''Watch it, Obie.

Point the damn gun up—push the wire down with it." Or, "Careful, Felix. When you eject the shells, be sure where the barrel is pointing."

In all the years that I knew Barney, I didn't once see him go through a stop sign or a red light. He didn't drive too fast or pass on a hill. He was so careful that he made me nervous. You have probably seen men who never leave their homes without mirror shines on their shoes or knife-blade presses in their pants. It is a kind of personality quirk that never varies. So it was with Barney Heffner. Being careful was his thing in life, a kind of subsectarian religion. That is why I was so sure that he didn't kill himself.

After the funeral, instead of returning to my office, I walked down to the Overland Hotel Coffee Shop, shivering a little in the gray November afternoon, musing over the Christian burial ceremonies, the pious mewing of the ministers, and the gut-tearing anguish of the family as their loved one sinks slowly into the ground amid incantations and fictitious eulogies. If my wife and kids put themselves through that insanity when I go, they will deserve it, because I have told them many times to burn me up and toss me into the Deerhorn.

In the coffee shop I saw some of the faces recently seen on that dreary hill of Hessberg Cemetery, and picking a booth, I sat down with the county attorney, Lenny O'Shay, and another young lawyer, Friedrich Wagmann, junior. I should tell you right here that Junior is a hell of a lot brighter than his old man, Friedrich Wagmann, senior. He is brighter than the county attorney, too, but that is to be expected. In our part of the country, at least, county attorneys are lawyers who can't quite make it in

private practice without some kind of subsidy.
What they do is run for office, and when they get
elected, spend most of their time in private practice. The counties provide them with offices and
salaries that are sometimes quite generous, so whatever they make in private practice is pure gravy.
Even a mediocre shyster can flourish under such
conditions. A lot of the county attorneys I know are
young men just out of college, or old men about
ready to throw in the towel. A few of them are
people like O'Shay, who just hasn't made the grade,
and never will. He has been our county attorney for
six years, primarily because nobody else wants to
run for it. Lenny gets ten grand, plus office and
secretary, and makes that much more on the side.
This is less than a good hustling lawyer can make in
Kornfeld County, according to my best information.
So his job is safe until some ambitious young dude
just out of college, or some ancient warrior facing
retirement decides to run for the office. Then we
may get a new county attorney.

"Been to the funeral?" Junior asked, moving his
big feet to let me slide in.

"Yeh," I said, looking around for my favorite
waitress, Sissy Borchers, who is not only good-
looking, but has a personality that won't quit. She
bubbles with charm and youthful vitality, and
smells like wild roses.

"Hello, Mr. Oberstdorf," she said, coming up fast
from the kitchen. "The usual?"

"Yes, ma'am," I replied in my best Dutch-uncle
manner. And she went behind the counter to get me
a cup of black coffee and a slice of green apple pie.

"A tragic accident," Lenny told us, shaking his
dark head sadly. "All those children, and that poor
woman alone now."

"It was no accident," I said, startling them both.

"No accident?" Wagmann asked, gazing at me with his round, pale-eyed face.

"What else could it be?" O'Shay demanded. "He was found draped over a fence with his shotgun—one shell fired and his belly blown away. Do you think he killed himself, Felix?"

"Nope."

Sissy was back with the pie and coffee. Writing my check, she inquired idly, "Is Heinie coming home for Christmas, Mr. Oberstdorf?"

"As far as I know, Sissy. We're planning on it."

"Well, tell him hello."

"Don't worry. He'll be around to see you, Miss Borchers. Old Heinie is not coming all the way up here for Christmas and not look up the prettiest girl in town."

Seeming to be pleased, she put my check down on the table and walked away to take an order at another booth.

The county attorney, frowning heavily, asked me why I thought that Barney Heffner had been murdered. It had him worried, I assumed, because if true, he might have to get to work on county business for a change.

"I didn't say he was murdered."

"You said it was no accident, and that he didn't kill himself. What then?"

"Maybe somebody else killed him accidentally."

"*What?*" big, blond Junior asked. "With Barney's own gun?"

"Almost. Somebody could have shot him accidentally, then discharged Barney's shotgun and left it there as a screen."

Wagmann was skeptical. "Isn't that pretty farfetched, Obie?"

"Of course it is. I was just clowning around. Actually, he *was* murdered."

Outside the plate glass window of the café, a leaden sky was lowering fast. We were in for one of our famous midwestern storms.

"An interesting theory," Lenny grunted, seeming to be disturbed by the thought of a murder in our county.

"It's more than a theory," I told him. "I've known old Barney most of my life, and he was Mr. Careful. The man would no more have shot himself than he would have blasted off to the moon in a spittoon."

O'Shay was still unconvinced. "If you are so sure he was murdered, who killed him?"

"I don't know, but I'm going to find out."

"Why *you*?" Junior asked. "Why not let the law handle it?"

Giving him a reproving glance, I scoffed, "Freddy, you know damn well the police in this county couldn't find their asses without a bloodhound and a squad of Pinkertons. I'll ask them, of course, and good old, grinning, back-slapping Hohenstein will squint and grunt and scratch his balls, then make some inane remark about the weather, and that will be the end of it. You know that as well as I do. The sheriff is all right for serving subpoenas or arresting speeders, but when it comes to real police work, he is lost. Besides, this is a personal thing with me. Nobody can gut-shoot a friend of mine, and leave him draped over a fence like some goddamned chicken-stealing coyote, and not make me mad! Who the hell does he think he is?"

"Who do *you* think he is?" Lenny asked, spooning his coffee absently.

"Somebody that Barney knew well...well enough to let him near, to blast him. See, the killer didn't have to use Barney's shotgun. He could have done it with any shotgun, then fired the shell that was in the chamber of Barney's gun, and then got some of Barney's blood on the barrel of the gun."

Wagmann shook his head. "I don't know, Obie. It sounds too complicated to me."

"Not at all," I assured him. "That is the only way it could have happened."

After finishing my pie and coffee in silence, I got up to leave, while they sat in embarrassment, sure that I was losing my reason but reluctant to say so. And they both knew that I knew what they were thinking, so we didn't have much left to talk about. Dropping a quarter onto the tablecloth for Sissy, I paid my check at the counter and walked out onto Colfax. It was twilight dark, and large, wet flakes of snow were spotting the sidewalk.

Starting west, I began thinking about people who might have wanted Barney dead, but couldn't come up with any. To my best knowledge, the little guy hadn't had an enemy in the world. But he must have had at least one, because your friends don't shoot you in the stomach with a shotgun and leave you hanging on a fence out in the boondocks.

Back in my office, I told the receptionist not to put through any calls to me for the rest of the day, and I sat at my desk for a long time, pondering the case, thinking idly about going out to see Milly Heffner and her children. After a half hour or forty-five minutes, I stepped into the outer office to ask Sara, my own private secretary, to type a relief order in the amount of twenty-five dollars for Milly. The amount was academic, because I knew that Milly

was not going to accept it anyway. Sara knew it,
too, but didn't say so. Sara, a severe, crinkle-faced
lady my own age, has never been married, and so
far as I know, has not even had a boyfriend. She is,
to use a much-abused cliché, wedded to her work.
The mousy little woman can really make a typewriter sing, and she knows more about the welfare
department than most social workers ever learn.
She knocked out the relief order before I could get
into my topcoat, and slipped it into a white envelope that had *Kornfeld County Welfare Department*
stamped in one corner. She smiled at me wanly, still
shaken by the death of her cousin, Barney Heffner.

"You tell Milly I'll be out there to see her in a day
or two," she ordered. "The poor little thing."

"Right."

We both knew that Milly would not need the relief order. Her old man, Klaus Borchers, is one of
the biggies mentioned earlier, not a multimillionaire
like John Braunholz or Dieter Emhoff, perhaps, but
one of the most prominent farmers in our part of
the country. He could have and would have set his
son-in-law up on a section of his own anytime, but
the son-in-law refused. He was a free soul, his own
man, until the day he died.

You hear people *oh-ing* and *ah-ing* all the time
about other people who are not living up to their
potential. Now and then you hear about a school
janitor with an I.Q. of one sixty-five, who should
really be teaching math or history in the school instead of mopping its floors—or a student seven feet
tall, who does not play basketball. People are dis-
mayed because these folks are not achieving. They
cry out, "Why doesn't he do something to use his
natural abilities?"

Thus, some people were very critical of Barney for not letting his father-in-law set him up in business on a big farm. But he didn't want to be a farmer, especially if he had to owe Klaus Borchers for it. He didn't want to feel like a kept man or a pimp. Old Barney did just what he wanted to do, when he wanted to do it. In a word, he was a free-lance truck driver. He had a Ford Big Six combination grain and stock truck, and he did a lot of hauling for both Emhoff and Braunholz. But they didn't own him. Nobody owned him. If the little fellow didn't feel like hauling, he didn't haul. They could just wait until tomorrow or get somebody else. If there happened to be a new snow, he'd go rabbit hunting, come hell or high water, and during deer season or pheasant season, he didn't haul anything for anybody. In the summer he spent a lot of time on the river, fishing for catfish and sturgeon, and he didn't ever let a July pass without spending a couple of weeks on some big lake in Canada. The man didn't owe anybody anything—tangible or intangible. His house and cars were paid for, and he didn't need or want any favors. On the day he died, hung up on a barbed-wire fence in Barrensen's pasture, he was even with the world, and it was strange that outside Kornfeld County, nobody knew that he was gone. It was strange because you get the feeling that people all over the world should have known about the passing of such a totally good, decent person.

When a hustler like John Braunholz or Dieter Emhoff cashes in, papers all over the state, even the prestigious *Winnebago City Star*, carry his obituary in a special box, like this: Prominent Businessman Dies In Hessberg. The obit then goes on to

list all his accomplishments and praise him as if he
were the departed Jesus Christ. The thing is that
there is a Braunholz or Emhoff in every county in
the United States. He is the aggressive, oily joiner
who would abuse his own grandmother for a dime,
and would not give you the time of day unless he
could write it off as a tax deduction. Braunholz
came out of the sticks in 1946 with five hundred
dollars cash that he got from the state as a veteran's
bonus. He parlayed that and a gift of gab into a
grain elevator paid for with federal money. He
stored federal grain in it at a dime a bushel until it
was paid for, then got Uncle Sam to build him some
more elevators, so that he could store some more
federal grain and make some more money. Next, he
bought 6,000 acres of farmland and put most of it
into the land bank, which means that Uncle Sam
eventually paid for the acreage. Emhoff played a
similar game, but inherited most of his wealth.
These are the people who get the notice when they
pop off. You never hear much about the Barney
Heffners. But believe me, there is a Heffner for
every Braunholz or Emhoff.

Thinking this way, I drove up Ninth Street,
toward the Heffner house, which sat in a small
grove of walnut trees on a hill, near the end of the
road. The house was just below the entrance to
Hessberg City Park, a small acreage of picnic tables
and outdoor grills that capped the hilltop. As wet
snow had made the blacktop slick, I had to go the
last quarter mile in second gear, spinning the
wheels a bit from time to time.

Pulling into the yard, I noted that Barney's truck
was parked beside the house under a new tarp, and
that there was a green Buick sedan behind it. And,

there was something missing, something that I could not identify until I got out of my jalopy to knock on the door. Then it came to me. Shaky wasn't there, wagging his tail, grinning up at me in his congenial, beagle way. Where was the little rabbit dog?

Paula, sixteen, opened the door for me, looking red-eyed and drawn, still darkly lovely in her sorrow.

"Oh, Mr. Oberstdorf, come in." She closed the door quickly behind me to shut out the damp chill of the day. I wiped my feet carefully on a terry-cloth mat that was thrown down on the living-room rug. It was a sad house, steeped in the anguish of death, and I began to feel uneasy, a stranger in a sacred place.

Warily I proffered the relief order, which was politely declined. Milly and I both knew that it was a formal gesture and that she would not accept it, but the weepy, hollow-eyed widow was most gracious in rejecting it. Not so her gaunt, Plattdeutscher father who hovered nearby. Klaus Borchers glared at me, offended that anybody would have the temerity to offer alms to his daughter. "We don't need no charity, Felix!"

His wife, equally Nordic and weather-beaten, was less hostile. "Thank you very much, Mr. Oberstdorf, but we can manage. My husband will take care of everything."

"Oh," I croaked, at a loss for something intelligent to say. "Where's Shaky?" I gazed around the room, halfway expecting to see him dozing in a corner.

"We don't know," said Frank, who was eighteen, and a young copy of his father. "Shaky went with dad and didn't come back." The kid was sitting on a leather couch, next to a large picture of Barney, homely and friendly with his generous nose and lank, brown hair.

"Maybe somebody killed Shaky, too," I said stupidly.

The boy's eyes widened. "Do you think my dad was murdered?"

"Yes, I do."

"So do I, Mr. Oberstdorf. My father was very careful. He would never shoot himself that way."

"He might," Klaus told us. "We all get careless once in a while."

"Not my dad," Frank insisted, gazing coldly at his grandfather. "He would never cross a fence unless he had the shotgun across the middle strand, pointed away from himself!"

"Now, boy," the elder cajoled him, "don't get upset."

"Hell, I'm not upset! The world is upset. My dad is gone!"

"Don't swear at your grandfather," Milly said gently.

"I'm sorry," the boy muttered.

"Tomorrow is Saturday," I told the kid. "Maybe we could go out to look for Shaky. He might be caught in a coyote trap, or hung up in some wire."

"Do you think he'll freeze?" asked Ginny, a seventh-grader with shoulder-length, auburn hair.

"You silly goose," said her identical twin, Minny. "He won't freeze. Thirty-two is freezing, and it's only thirty-five on our outside thermometer."

"Well, maybe not," Ginny conceded, "but he'll get pretty damn cold out there in the snow."

"My, my," grandma clucked.

"She learns that stuff at school," Paula advised her grandmother. "We spend all that money to send them to a Lutheran school and all they learn is how to cuss."

"We learn more than that," Ginny said sullenly, "don't we, Min?"

"Sure we do. We learn how to pray."

"Praise the Lord," chanted Ginny.

"Amen," Minny added.

The spiritual ascension of the family, however brief, was my clue to leave. Reminding Frank that I'd be over to pick him up the next morning, I got out of the little house, into my car, and onto the black strip of Ninth Street, thinking all the while about the formula for leaving a secure family when you head for that great welfare department in the sky. When my kids were growing up, I conned myself into believing that all a child really needs is a lot of love and a lot of discipline, that if one gives a kid a strong mind and a strong body as a gift of heredity, he needs no more to weather the storms of life. I convinced myself that if one teaches his children to live by the golden rule, sees them through school, it is all the start they need. Now, it seems to me that if one leaves his family with wealthy, loving grandparents, the other things may not be necessary.

## 2

IT IS A WEEKEND RITUAL of many years' standing with me. My good wife, Ellen, gets up early, starts my bathwater, and cooks breakfast while I am bathing. Some people who know about this phase of my life are very critical, sometimes openly so, but it doesn't bother me. If my wife wishes to run my bathwater, it is her business and mine. It is not that I am too lazy to get up and do it, but just that it is a luxury that I can enjoy. It is not as if she had to pump the water from a deep well and heat it over a wood-burning stove. All she has to do is turn a handle on the water pipe, then a few minutes later, turn it again, in the opposite direction. I would do it for her if she would ask. Some men who snicker about my letting my wife run my bathwater allow their wives to shovel snow and mow the lawn. One townsman who would not dream of such a thing has had his wife working in a laundry since the day after they got back from their honeymoon in 1952. One jackass who finds humor in my bathing habits hasn't seen a bath for years. But if my peers find humor in the situation, so be it. To each his own.

After my morning ablutions I go to the kitchen, where Ellen has a large hotcake and three eggs waiting for me on a plate, with a cup of coffee and a rasher of bacon on the side. While eating, I look over the *Morning Star* and turn on a transistor radio to get the latest news and weather report. This is what we call living it up in Hessberg on a weekend morning. By the time I've finished eating my eggs, the newspaper has been scanned from front to back. Then she puts another hotcake onto my plate, and after buttering and syruping it, I eat it, and have another cup of coffee before reading the want ads. In the want ads I look for business opportunities, cheap land and good jobs that I can qualify for. To be honest about it, job hunting is a kind of mental titillation, because a person with my qualifications is just about dead-ended. True, I have had twenty-five years of experience in social work, but am possessed of only a bachelor's degree in an era when higher degrees are just about required. In addition to that, I am approaching an age when most people are thinking more about retirement than about starting new jobs.

After scanning the ads, I work the crossword puzzle—not much challenge when you have been doing it for so many years. You eventually learn all the code words and clichés. You learn that a three-letter word for "vandal" is "hun," although in truth, a vandal was no more like a hun than a rooster is like a jar of grape jelly. But one thing I like about the *Star* puzzles is that they are old, like me. Most of them must be devised by people my age, because the movie star in forty-five across is always somebody like Adolphe Menjou or Myrna Loy. That gives me some advantage.

Anyhow, when the squares are all filled in, I carry the little transistor to the bathroom, where I shave, brush my teeth, and put in my partial plate. Only then am I ready to start the day.

When I came out of the bathroom to put on my boots and parka in the old-fashioned foyer, Ellen asked, "Where are you going so early?" and I said that I was going out to look for Barney's dog.

She seemed a little surprised. "Why you? Are you the official dogcatcher now? What about the game?"

She was talking about the football game on television at one-thirty. I had a small bet down on the outcome, as she knew. And when I have a bet down on a game, I like to watch the game if I can. As a matter of fact, I try to get a bet down on any game that is being televised, in order to make the game more fun to watch. It is not that I like to gamble.

My wife had a theory about Shaky's disappearance. "He probably found a girl friend and stayed over for a few days. He'll come home like Little Bo Peep's sheep, dragging his tail behind him."

"That's what I'd like to do sometime," I told her, "find a girl friend and stay over for a few days."

"Hah, what would you do for a few days?"

Ignoring that, I went outside where the sun was shining brightly and the snow was nearly gone from the streets. Following me out to the porch, she asked, "Just in case somebody calls for you, what time will you be home?"

"Before the game starts," I assured her, and got into my car and drove north toward the Heffner house. When I got there, I found the kid waiting outside. By ten minutes past ten, we were crossing the river, headed for the place where his dad had been found.

The Deerhorn River splits our county into two distinct entities, one known as East River, the other, not surprisingly, called West River. East River is pure midwest, with rich, rolling farmlands, while West River is a region of arid plateaus and deep canyons, fit only for livestock grazing and antelope hunting.

Once across the rumbling, steel arch bridge, we turned north onto Interstate 90 to skirt the great escarpment for a mile and a half before turning sharply left, up a steep, gravel road to the high plateau. A mile past the crest of the hill, Frank ordered, "Pull up here, Mr. Oberstdorf. It's over there by the gate." He pointed at a split-rail gate that closed a gap in a barbed-wire fence. "Doug Barrensen found dad there, about ten yards to the left of the gate."

Getting out of the car, we walked slowly across a thin layer of snow to the fence and stood looking at the place. The earth was covered with clean snow, which masked whatever bloodstains might have been on the grass before, and there was no sign of blood on the rusty wire of the fence.

"Jesus, it's cold up here," the kid said, shivering in his light jacket.

He was right, it was colder up there than down in the valley, because we were six hundred feet higher. Gazing eastward, we could see the town, cupped in Boneyard Valley. A few hundred yards from the river, we could see the sweep of the prairie and the grain fields beyond.

"Why would he cross the fence thirty feet from the gate," Frank demanded of me, "when all he had to do was either climb over the gate or open it. It is never locked."

"He wouldn't," I replied. "It would have been too easy to just pull the gate open and walk through. Do you have any idea as to who might have wanted to see him dead—some disgruntled business contact or somebody like that?"

The boy shook his head slowly from side to side. "Nope, he didn't have an enemy in the world—that I know of. He wasn't a pushy man, Mr. Oberstdorf. All he ever did was fish and hunt and haul enough cattle and corn to earn us a living. I didn't ever know anybody that didn't like dad."

"I didn't either, Frankie. Your father was one of the finest men that I have ever known. Is it possible that he caught somebody shooting a deer out of season? Would he blow the whistle, threaten to turn the person in?"

Frankie thought about it for a while. "Possibly. But there are no deer up here. They're all down in the valley where the good browse is."

"Antelope?"

"Not likely. You have to get farther in before you see any antelope. Anyway, dad was not a crusader. He was satisfied to let the game wardens do their work."

"Okay, let's rule that out for the time being. What other motives could there be—robbery?"

The youth laughed shortly. "My old man never carried more than three dollars in his pocket as long as I knew him. Anyway, he had still had his billfold and money on him when he was found."

I tried again. "All right, what about the man who found him—Doug Barrensen?"

"Negative. He's dad's first cousin. They grew up together and went into the service together. They were like brothers."

All the while we were talking, we were walking through scrub oak and sagebrush along the rim of a canyon that cut into the mesa from the river, a result of centuries of erosion and rock slides.

"There's something down there," Frank said, stopping to point into the depths. "See there, just below that big rock, see that black spot?"

I saw it, a hundred feet below us, sheltered from the north wind, but not from the sun. It looked like a patch of bare earth in the snow, but as we stared, it began to look more and more like a small black and white dog. Finding a path, we scrambled down to the spot where Shaky lay huddled. There was a tiny, red hole in the top of his head, where somebody had planted a twenty-two caliber slug. There was blood matted in the hair of his head and on the floppy ears, as if Shaky had not died at once, but had survived long enough to shake his head in an effort to dislodge the stinger. Silently, shocked by the significance of it, we covered the dead beagle with chunks of sandstone and slabs of shale before returning to the rim of the fissure.

"Let's go home," Frank said, choking with rage. "I have to figure this out."

So there wasn't any doubt about it. Barney had been murdered and so had his dog. Young Heffner and I remained silent until we were across the river, driving along Colfax toward Ninth, where I asked, "What are you going to tell your mother?"

"Nothing for a while. She's out at the farm—took the girls out there to get away from the house for a few hours. The house is a sad place, Mr. Oberstdorf."

"Yes, I suppose so. What you are going to do about your dad's business—are you going to work the truck?"

He shrugged as we pulled into his yard. "I'm not sure. I'd like to, but gramps wants to send me to ag college. Mom and the girls will be getting some social security and V.A. benefits. Dad was drawing a disability compensation from Korea."

"I know."

"Come on in," he said, getting out of my car.

"Okay." I followed the kid into his house, where he put a pan of water on the kitchen stove to heat.

"Maybe we should give the sheriff a call," Frank suggested.

"What for?"

"To report the murder." His forehead was knitted tightly.

Gazing at the youngster, feeling his anguish, I told him, "Normally, I'd say yes,but in this case it seems like a pure waste of time. It might be better to contact the highway patrol."

Actually, I have always been critical of movies and television shows where the victim of a crime, or his advocate, does everything but what he should do—call the police. Somebody turns up dead, or is reported missing, and his family gets involved with a private detective or an insurance adjuster, or some such unlikely authority, or just handle it themselves. And by some miracle, it usually comes out all right in the end. If you will just analyze most of these so-called mystery stories, you will quickly see that if the cops had been called in the first place, there would have been no mystery and no story. And of course, the story is the thing.

But in this case, asking for help from the obvious authority figure, Sheriff Kurt Hohenstein, would have been a sheer waste of time. Like many elected officials, old Kurt is just plain incompetent. See, the way it is, you don't have to pass an I.Q. test to run for an office. Nor do you have to be capable, honest or reliable. All you have to do is pay your filing fee, then go out and corral enough votes to get you in. It helps to have a gift of gab, an imposing appearance, and a little money for campaign expenses. Kurt has all these, plus hundreds of clannish relatives all over the county. And even those kinfolk who know him for the fourteen-carat phony that he is will vote for him, just to keep the job in their family. He may be a big counterfeit, but he is *their* counterfeit.

The sheriff is a large, dark, movie-star-handsome man, with a hearty backslap and breezy howdy for everybody he meets. The suntan western hat that all bona fide sheriffs in the United States of America wear is a natural prop for old Kurt, because he just looks for all the world like a typical, western-type cowboy hero. You know, the two-fisted, straight-shooting chap seen in late television movies. He has been sheriff of Kornfeld County for seven years, and is good for God knows how many more.

Coming out of my reverie, I asked the kid, "Is it all right if I take a look at some of your dad's things, Frank?"

"Sure, it might lead to something. He had a kind of office-library in the basement, where he kept his guns, fishing tackle and rock collection—things that he was interested in."

Going downstairs behind him I asked, "Rock collection?"

"Sure, whenever he was out hunting or fishing, he'd pick up pretty or unusual rocks and bring them home. He collected pieces of jade, agate, lava—all that stuff. Heck, he even brought home a lump of coal one time."

"Coal?"

"Yeah, coal. Here, take a look at this." Reaching into a box of rock specimens at one side of the room, he pulled out a piece of coal about the size of my fist.

Why would Barney have been interested in coal? He had an oil furnace. Anyway, you can buy a lump of coal in a lumberyard or pick one up on the railroad tracks. Why would he carry home a little piece of coal and give it a place among his valued rock samples?

In response to the sounds of water boiling over onto a fire, my host ran upstairs to take his water off the heat, and then I smelled the aroma of brewing coffee. Waiting for Frank to bring the beverage down, I shuffled through some letters that his dad had left on an end table. There was advertising matter from gun companies and insurance agencies, as well as travel brochures from several tourist bureaus. Among all this promotional material was a nine-by-twelve envelope from the Department of the Interior. Inside I found a booklet explaining the Homestead Act of 1862. Why would Barney have been interested in that stuff? He didn't care anything about farming. He once told me that he had all the farming he wanted while growing up on his father's place. Thus, his apparent interest in homesteading was a puzzler to me.

In another envelope there was a small pamphlet, *Mining Claims—Questions and Answers*, also published by the United States Department of the Interior, Bureau of Land Management.

I asked Frank about these things, expressing my surprise that his dad would be interested in such material.

"Heck, he was interested in everything," the boy said, pointing at one wall of the room that was covered from floor to ceiling with books. "Did you know that he was an authority on Albert Schweitzer?"

When I admitted my ignorance of that side of his father, he told me about it. "Dad put Schweitzer in a class with Leonardo da Vinci as one of the great men of all time. He read all the books about Schweitzer that he could get his hands on. Would you believe that he drove all the way to Winnebago one time, just to buy a new book about the man? He even asked the Hessberg City Council to erect a monument to Schweitzer on the courthouse lawn He told them that every German-American community should have a statue of the greatest German of the century."

"German? I thought that Schweitzer was French."

"Hah, French nothing. He was born in Alsace and German was his mother tongue. During World War I, he was barred from France as an enemy alien. Did you know that he was not only a theology student and writer, but an organist, organ builder, and an authority on the life of Bach, before he went into medicine?"

"Do tell," I murmured.

The kid laughed self-deprecatingly. "I'm beginning to sound like dad. But when he got an idea into his head, he just would not give up on it. Like the time he got interested in uranium. He just about lived in the city park."

"The park? Why the park, with all that space across the river to explore?"

The kid shrugged. "Don't ask me. I don't know."

"Did he ever find any uranium?"

"Not that I know of. He finally got onto some other kick and forgot about uranium. I think his Geiger counter is out in the garage, with some of his other mementos of fantasyland."

I was curious about the uranium hunt. "When was all that going on?"

"Two or three years ago, before he got on the Schweitzer thing."

This information was a bit puzzling, considering that the letters from Washington had been received within the past month. Obviously something had been rekindled in Barney to cause an interest in public lands.

Pigeonholing that line of thought for the time being, I asked Frank whether he planned to move out to his grandfather's farm.

"Not for the present. I'll probably do some hauling until after Christmas, then enroll in college. Mom and the girls will stay on here at least until the end of the school year. They may not move at all. Dad left fifty thousand dollars worth of insurance. That would set mom up in business. She has always wanted to raise Rock Cornish chickens for market. We have four acres behind the house. She may build a big chicken house out there." He stopped talking, seeming to be uncertain about what he was saying.

Looking at me almost pleadingly, Frank asked, "Are we going to catch the one who did it, Mr. Oberstdorf?"

"If it is the last thing I ever do," I promised.

A promise is a promise, but how do you deliver on something like that? How do you find a person who has no name, no form, no odor or substance—who is just a ghost or a figment of your imagination? Sure, I do a lot of investigating in my work. The welfare department has to check the banks to see that welfare applicants do not have money hidden away. There are home calls and telephone calls.

Letters are written and neighbors quizzed. Employers are contacted. But that is not the way to look for an unknown killer. Or is it? The techniques are basic. You ask questions and collate the answers.

You start with the murder weapon, for instance, and assume that it was a twenty-two caliber rifle or pistol. You assume that the killer shot Barney in the belly with a twenty-two, then blew him apart with his own shotgun to make it look like a hunting accident. An educated guess is that the dog tried to defend his master, was shot and tossed into the canyon hastily.

There are four thousand people living in Kornfeld County, half of them men or boys, each with his own twenty-two rifle or pistol. All you have to do is check out each of them to find out who was out on the mesa when Barney was killed. He could be the killer. That is silly, of course, but it points up the problem.

"Let's start a program of elimination," I said. "Maybe the killer was a homicidal maniac on leave from the state hospital. Maybe he got a gun, killed your father, and then checked back into the hospital. I'll go out to the hospital Monday and check it out—find out whether any of their dangerous patients were away from the place when your dad was killed."

Frank looked skeptical. "I don't want to offend you, Mr. Oberstdorf, but that seems like a remote possibility."

"Right, it is remote, but we have to start someplace. Maybe there is some kind of clue at the funny farm that we are not aware of just now."

It was time to leave. The football game would be coming on in less than an hour, and I needed some beer and pretzels to share the opening kickoff. I'd have to stop someplace on my way home and get three or four quarts. Normally I'd have bought them at a grocery store to save some money, but having embarked upon an investigation, I thought that it might be a good idea to get with some people. If you plan to investigate somebody, you must talk to other bodies. That being the case, there is no place in Hessberg like a saloon, where alcohol loosens tongues. And in Hessberg, the biggest saloon is Pete's Place, sixty feet square, with a circle bar that is surrounded by forty stools and thirteen tables. Pete's is not the only bar in town by a long shot, but is the one that everybody visits on occasion, as it's right on the main drag and near a state highway. When I walked in, Peter Austerheim, the owner and head bartender grunted: "Hi, Obie, where you been? I haven't seen you lately."

"That's because I haven't been in lately."

"Why not—don't you like me anymore?"

"I like you fine, but I can't afford you. Every time the state raises taxes a dime on a case of beer, you go up a nickel on a bottle. When the brewery goes up a buck on a barrel of beer, you go up a dime on a pitcher of suds. Grocery stores don't do that. They absorb it. I can buy a quart of beer in the store for fifty cents. You charge seventy-five. Give me a stein and a package of cashews."

Smiling amiably, the rangy redhead drew my beer, letting the foam build up on top just the way it should. Some people don't like a heavy collar on their beer, but without an adequate layer of foam, the brew gets flat in a hurry.

"If we had more penny pinchers like you in town," Pete complained, "I'd go busted."

"You'll go busted," I scoffed, "when the Deer-horn River runs uphill."

The truth is that old Pete is just as glad that I don't go into his place more often. He does a pretty good business with welfare recipients, and he knows that if I were hanging around, they wouldn't be. Aside from that, we have done each other a few favors in the past, so whether I buy beer from him or not is a matter of small concern to him. Whatever he charges for beer and booze, Pete will always have customers, because he runs a nice place and is competitive. If every bar in town would double their prices, business would not fall off ten percent, because alcoholism is a creature of loneliness. And lonely people will drink in public places, whatever it costs.

Farmers in big hats and muddy boots were drift-ing in to get good seats for the football game. They came in jovially, greeting and slapping each other in good fellowship, squatting in threes and fours at tables around pitchers of beer and shots of booze. They were temporarily emancipated from the oner-ous rounds of slopping hogs, milking cows, and hauling manure out of barns.

One of them, Jay Clements, called out, "Hey, Obie, did you catch the bad man?"

He was at a table with Bud Adamek and Feikke Klasterer, who both whinnied at his little joke. They all stared at the half-Indian waitress who car-ried a pitcher of beer to a corner table, holding it out at arm's length to keep it from splashing her chest.

"Wow!" Jay cried. "Look at that big pitcher of beer!"

That of course brought more laughter from Bud

and Feikke, who may have stopped someplace else before honoring Pete with their presence.

"Let's drink one more pitcher of beer," Jay giggled, "then go out and help Obie catch that mean old killer!"

"First we watch the game," Feikke replied, letting go a loud belch. "I ain't going noplace until after Big Blue wins a game. If they win this one, they get a bowl bid."

Coming to the bar with an empty pitcher, Jay told me, "I got my rifle in my car, Obie, if you want to go hunting killers."

You may get some idea of how it is in small towns. You tell the county attorney something one day, and it is all over town within twenty-four hours. It may even come back to you in comic form. O'Shay is just the peanut brain to pass it off as a joke.

"If somebody killed Barney, I hope to Christ his soul burns in hell. If you have any evidence at all, Felix, you should give it to the state patrol. They have a homicide division. Don't leave it to Kurt and that goofy county attorney.... Speak of the devil, there is our esteemed sheriff now!" The bar owner frowned.

And indeed it was—old Kurt Hohenstein himself, cowboy hat and all, filling up the doorway of the joint. Spotting me, he came right over, grinning and slapping as usual. "Hi, there, Felix. What are you drinking?"

Instead of arguing, I accepted a stein of beer, and pushing the big hat back to show off his wavy hair, the sheriff tossed a Kennedy half-dollar onto the bar. Straddling a stool, he poured a cup of hot coffee from a Silex pot that sat on an electric warmer near the service bar.

"How is your investigation going?" he asked
jovially, careful to not sound flippant. People who
depend upon the ballot for their bread and butter
soon learn how to be jovial without being flippant.

"We found Barney's dog in a canyon, with a hole
in his head," I answered. "It looks as if the dog
might have tried to defend his boss. The hole looked
about the size of a twenty-two. The way I figure it,
somebody shot Barney in the stomach with a
twenty-two, then blew away the evidence with a
shotgun—or killed him with a shotgun, then fired
Barney's gun to make it look like an accident."

He assumed a thoughtful expression. "Maybe I'd
better have a look at the dog, Felix."

"We buried him under rocks."

"We?" He peered at me anxiously.

"Frankie Heffner and me."

"Oh. Maybe I'd better get the kid to take me out
there—after the game."

"Whatever you want to do," I said, shrugging.

"By the way," he said, looking past me at the
waitress, "your statement to O'Shay about the murder is all over the county by now."

"I know. What about it?"

"Well, if Barney really was murdered, the killer
may try to shut you up before you can identify him."

"I sure hope so, Kurt, because unlike old Barney,
I do not love and trust everybody. The first stranger
who looks at me cross-eyed is in serious trouble."
Pulling back the front of my parka, I gave the
sheriff a look at my automatic pistol, and brimming
over with rage, I told him, "I pray to God that the
murdering bastard tries something with me!"

"Don't do anything rash, Obie," he advised me.
"I'm on the case."

"That doesn't mean that I'm *off* it. Give me three quarts of Martz to go, Pete, and a sack of pretzels. I'm going home to watch the game. If Big Blue does right by me, I'll win ten bucks."

As I was leaving, Kurt called after me, "If you come up with anything else, let me know, Obie."

"Sure."

He leaned back against the bar to look at the half-Indian girl, who returned his gaze of admiration. It was easy to see that they had something going between them. Outside, I took a deep breath of the warm afternoon and headed for home, walking quickly. When I got there, Ellen had lunch ready— nothing big, just a Reuben sandwich and a big slice of hot apple pie with coffee. After eating, I turned the TV on and put a heavy chunk of walnut into the fireplace, because it was colder in the house than outside in the sunlight. A big wad of newspapers under the log was enough to get a nice fire going once I lighted it. The flames licked up around the walnut wood slowly, igniting it in several places, and before long there was a pleasant fire burning. The flames, framed in a granite and brass archway, took the chill off, allowing me to watch the game in comfort, and two undefeated elevens were getting teed up to play an exciting game for me. But suddenly, I was lonely and dreary as I remembered the days when my boys were with me to watch the Saturday afternoon games, and before that, the Friday night high-school games. Earl and Heinie were a long way off, one with the army in Germany, the other at a college in the South. Their faces stared at me out of a twin frame atop the fireplace mantel, Heinie, fair and smiling, Earl, dark and serious, obviously concerned about something behind the camera. The gold bars of his second lieutenancy shone proudly on his squared shoulders. Crossed rifles on his lapels reminded me of my own unhappy career in the United States Army. Well, they were coming home for Christmas, so it wasn't an occasion for great sorrow to be watching the game alone.

As I thought about the boys, a football player in a blue uniform rushed up to kick the ball off the tee, and the game was on.

**3**

ON SUNDAY MORNING after breakfast, I took a walk, something that I do frequently because I like to do it. Some people get the same physical joy from walking that others do from smoking or sipping brandy. It is a great pleasure to use one's legs, to glory in the feel of the earth beneath one's feet, to breathe deeply of the country air. It is possible to see things while walking that you don't see while driving—birds fluttering in juniper bushes, children playing cowboys and Indians around their imaginary covered wagons, neighborhood matrons peering out their picture windows in search of gossip items. When walking you can hear the heartbeat of a community, smell its baking cakes and percolating coffee. People who don't walk miss a lot in life. Yet how many of us will jump into a car, to drive a few blocks for a package of cigs or a six-pack of beer? How many red-blooded Americans do you know who will risk a parking ticket rather than walk a few blocks to a business appointment? In Hessberg very few people walk anyplace, although it is easy to walk from one end of town to the other in fifteen minutes. I've hiked ten thousand miles within the city limits, and a walk is always a new experience for me. I have been walking around and running around in the community since age five, when my father returned from a hitch in the navy and brought me back home. In my case, walking is learning, and much of my hiking is on the job as I go from welfare home to welfare home. I meet all the old folks, the sick people and the abandoned wives and underprivileged children, as well as delinquent fathers. Because most of my clients have relatives scattered around the county, every application for assistance is an introduction to a new tribe, or at least a reintroduction. And I have contacts with all the official helping agencies—Division of Employment, Vocational Rehabilitation, Social Security, Veterans' Service Office and others, local and regional. In addition, the welfare department deals directly with doctors, lawyers, dentists, pharmacists, nursing home operators and grocers, to name a few. So, if walking is a pleasure with me, it is also my business.

My Sunday walk took me to the home of Thaddeus Miller, age ninety-seven, an old-age assistance recipient as well as a veteran of the Spanish-American War. Please believe me when I tell you that only a murder investigation would get me into his house voluntarily, although I do go there occasionally on business. The old man does not change clothes very often or bathe religiously. There are empty soup cans scattered about the floor of the one-room shack, obsolete newspapers, moldy with years, stacked against all four walls. His bed is a great blob of soiled blankets and patchwork quilts.

"If you came here to get me for the insane asylum," he greeted me, quavering with anger, "forget it, kid! I told you that before, a thousand times."

Looking at him sternly, I told him, "It wasn't a

thousand times, Mr. Miller, it was twice. And it wasn't the insane asylum, it was a nursing home. But that's not what I'm here for. What I'm here for is to ask you something about the coal mine."

"What coal mine?"

"What coal mine do you suppose? The one that you worked in for twenty-six years—the one that closed down ten years ago."

"Oh, *that* coal mine. I don't know anything about that mine. Hell, I only worked there. When I was a kid, we used to shovel coal out of the ground like corn out of a crib. Why, my daddy never burned anything but coal the first sixteen years after we moved here from Wisconsin."

"Listen," I said, "why don't you get a shave and a haircut? You look like a doggone polar bear with that dirty white blanket all over your head and face. Or at least you could wash it—get the tobacco juice out of it. Dollars to doughnuts you're lousy."

"No, I'm not," he said haughtily, "but I was once—in 1898 in Cuba. I'll never forget it, Obie."

"Hey! How can you remember something so trivial as having had lice in 1898? That sounds like a lot of bull to me!"

"I can remember plenty," he said. "I remember Teddy Roosevelt and San Juan Hill."

"Come off it, you old fraud. You didn't ever *see* Teddy Roosevelt or San Juan Hill."

Like a lot of Spanish-American War heroes, old Thad saw most of his action in the bars and bordellos of Tampa, Florida, but it was enough to get him a small, non-service-connected pension to augment his old-age assistance benefits. He could live in a nice nursing home, or better yet, in Midwest State Hospital, where old folks are treated so well that you wouldn't believe it. But he is a testy old warrior who wouldn't move out of his miserable hog wallow to go live in the governor's mansion.

Every now and then, I slip up the hill to Thad's place with a few dainties in a brown paper sack—a bottle of wine, or a pint of ice cream, a pound of fresh grapes or a six-pack of suds—things that he enjoys but doesn't normally buy for himself. And I suppose the truth is that he is one of my favorite people, with his old-time fire and independence. For that matter, I hold age in respect, feeling that old folks deserve some kind of consideration just for being around so long. Besides, assuming that they are as smart as anybody else, they should know more, having had longer to learn things. So I enjoy talking to elders, especially the salty ones like Thad Miller.

"Where did you and your father dig all that easy coal, Thad?"

"What coal?"

"The coal that you burned when you came out here from Wisconsin."

"Pleasure before business," he replied. "What did you bring me?" He sat down wearily in a sagging leather chair that had horsehair stuffing hanging out of it in a dozen places. The old man seemed to shrink up, gnomelike, in his floppy overalls.

"A pint of Old Crow," I replied, bringing the flat bottle out of my jacket. "What about the coal?"

Before handing over the whiskey, I cracked the seal, knowing that he would have trouble with it, and taking the bottle from me, he tipped it up to take a long pull at it. Lowering the pint, he gasped. "Boy, I really like that bonded hooch, kid. It's nice and hot."

"The coal," I reminded him.

"Up on the hill by the Indian mission. The damn Indians didn't use it. They burned wood. Hell, I had a sharp ax and a mule, and I would trade a mule-load of wood for a girl. Man, if you ain't never spent a night with one of them Cedar Ridge Indian girls, kid, you ain't never lived!" Rolling his faded eyes, he took another pull at the Old Crow. "Christ, you may think that you are crazy, Oberstdorf, but I was really goofy in them days. Why, I used to chop wood all day, and trade it for an hour in a tepee. I wanted to marry one of them girls, but I wasn't rich enough. Her old man wanted ten horses, and all I had was one spavined old mule, blind in one eye and mean as hell. That was in 1900. Or was it 1901?" He stared up at me uncertainly.

Thaddeus Miller is not only the oldest person in Hessberg, but the most outrageous storyteller. With him you never know where fact leaves off and fiction begins. Chances are that he himself does not know.

"*What* mission?" I demanded, beginning to get annoyed with the old man's malarkey.

He gazed at me reprovingly. "There was only one, Obie, the Moravian Brethren Mission up on the hill." He jerked a thumb over his shoulder toward the park up at the top of Ninth Street. "They built a church out of cottonwood slabs, with a bell tower on top. Then they got a bell and put a long rope on it. The bell was cast in Solingen—that's in Germany—in 1796. By the time it got here, the Indians was about ready to move out. When Reverend Madgeburg started pulling on the rope, you could hear it all up and down the valley, and the doggone Indians and all the other people that wasn't Lutherans or Catholics, came running to see what was happening.'' He paused for another pull at the bottle, then continued. "What was happening most of the time was that the Moravians had a great big pot of stew simmering out in the yard, and they had piles of fresh-baked bread on a wagon bed. After the service, they all ate and sang songs.''

"After the service?''

"That's what I said. What's the matter, don't you hear good—or don't you believe me? There never was no such thing as a free lunch, kid. If you want to dine, you got to whine!''

I sighed, having been turned away from my point, and asked my old friend, "What about the coal, Mr. Miller?''

"Jesus Christ, Obie, you keep running off at the head while I'm trying to give you a history lesson. I'm telling you about the goddamned church! The bell is out in my backyard.''

"What?''

The elder took a final swig of the pint bottle then held it upside down to be sure that there wasn't anything left. "I said it's out in my backyard—the old church bell. If you want it, you can have it. I'm getting on in years, Oberstdorf. Another ten or fifteen years and I'll be gone. Ashes to ashes and dust to dust, kid, just another little stone in the graveyard. You're so interested in that Moravian mission, I'm going to give you the bell.''

"I'm not—'' I began.

"Come on,'' he said, jerking himself up out of the chair, gasping with the effort, "before I change my mind and give it to the damn Luther League.''

Everybody in Hessberg knew about Miller's bells, mostly junk collected from church steeples up and

down the valley. Anytime a church burned, blew
down or simply gave way to the ravages of time,
Old Man Miller cabbaged onto the bell and got somebody with a truck to haul it in. There were big bells
and little bells, brass bells and iron bells, pretty
bells and ugly bells. Besides church bells, he had
behind his tiny house cowbells and steamboat bells,
and even a bell from a locomotive, circa 1840.

"I promised them to the Luther League when I
die," he once told me, "because I don't want the
damn county to get them. The county can have my
house and my pistol, but not the doggone bells.
They'd sell the bells to some junkyard in Winnebago
City for scrap. Then somebody would melt them
down to make doorstops or spittoons out of them."

He led me out of the house, through a patch of
dead weeds that left stickers on my clothes. His
bells were scattered about the yard in waist-high
weeds, resting on wooden platforms, some of which
were rotting with age. A relic of a horse-drawn
wagon, its crumbling wheels in two feet of dirt and
grass, held a load of bells, large and small. Beside
the wagon, resting on a heavy plank that was sup-
ported by two sawhorses, was a brass bell four feet
high.

"There she is," Thad told me proudly, "the old
mission bell."

A conga line of angels with round faces and stub-
by wings danced around the bottom edge of the
bell, and near the top where a rope was supposed to
tie in was a small inscription stamped into the
metal. Peering closely, I could make out the letters
and numbers—Solingen—1796.

"Well, I'll be doggoned," I said. "Isn't that *something*?"

"I'm not kidding," the elder assured me. "You come up here with a truck and get the bell. I never gave you nothing, Oberstdorf, and you're a good kid." Gazing up the hill toward the park, he told me, "The mission was up there, right on that hill. The coal vein was halfway down to the river on the west side. We dug it out by hand until one day the whole damn hillside caved in. The Moravian Church still owns the hill. They bought it from the Indians in 1895."

I was puzzled. "Are you talking about the city park?"

"City park nothing! That land belongs to the Moravian Church, and if it don't, I'll kiss your ass on the fourth of July at noon on the main street of town!" His eyes grew large in anger and excitement.

The whole thing was surprising to me, that a bit of local history of such significance could have been forgotten in such a short period of time. The commercial coal mine was located three miles east of town, four miles from the park. Wouldn't one suppose that old-timers might have told the mining company about the coal on the hill and that they would have tried to mine it? Or was it investigated and found to be commercially not feasible? At any rate, I did not recall hearing any such talk when the mine closed in the middle sixties. Maybe Thad was pulling my leg. But then, he told me about the bell, and there *was* a bell. If there was a bell, maybe there was a mission, and if there was a mission, maybe there was a vein of coal. Whatever the facts, they had to be verified, for my own peace of mind as well as for the pursuit of my investigation. So, bidding my elderly friend goodbye, I started up

toward the park, hiking along the blacktop of Ninth
Street past the Heffner house, which looked deserted
with only the truck still in the yard to indicate
human habitation. The family was, I assumed, still
out at the Borchers's farm.

Under my parka the hard steel of my automatic
rubbed my rib cage, and I caught myself hoping that
somebody would follow me to the park and try
something with me, because it would be the most
simple way to solve the case. We could just shoot it
out.

The street climbs steeply up to the park gate to
end there at a framework of peeled logs that serves
as the entranceway. A small mound of cemented
rocks beside the gate has a smooth face of cement
with a simple message on it—Hessberg City
Park—1900. The flattened top of the hill, an acre in
extent, is circled by a gravel road, with space
around the outside circumference for parking. Sitting in a parked car you can look out over the town,
which is only about one square mile in extent. The
only structures in town more than two stories high
are the courthouse dome, two church spires and the
Braunholz grain elevators. The community television tower, three hundred feet tall, is on the rim of
the mesa, a mile west of town. That puts it up there
above us some nine hundred feet, enough for good
reception from stations in Win City and Omaha.
There is a microwave transmitter at the tower. It
relays the pictures to us, giving us the same kind of
viewing that our friends in the cities get.

Below the parking area, on the river side, the hill
is heavily wooded, clear to the water, a half mile
distant. This is deer and rabbit country, and every
so often you hear about a hunter killing a bobcat.

Mountain lions and timber wolves left with the Indians and the buffalo, but coyotes and foxes, as well as raccoons, abound in the woods on the east bank of the big river, and for some years, naked-tailed opossums have been extending their range northward along the Deerhorn. East of the river, in rolling farmlands of corn and hay, pheasants and prairie chicken do well, and on occasion one may get a shot at a turkey.

This is not meant to be a zoological report, but does explain, in part, the world of Barney Heffner, who did most of his hunting east of the river, going west only for antelope and jack rabbits. He liked to hunt up on the mesa once in a while, he had told me, to get the feel of the west, to shake off the confinement of space in a region where one ranch might cover a hundred square miles, where one could drive fifty miles without seeing a town, a filling station or a paved road.

A path meandered down from the knob through clumps of blue spruce and sumac trees toward the river. The lower I went, the heavier the growth and the taller the trees, until halfway down, I found myself in a twilight world of great oaks and thick underbrush. Blundering through the forest, I came upon a fresh erosion, the result of heavy rains during recent weeks before the weather changed. It was a great cup in the hillside that did not boast of large trees, but only of less imposing timber of more recent growth—that is to say, trees fifty or sixty years old. Normally this type of terrain does not erode even under the worst rainfall conditions. In our part of the country heavy rains are rare. Erosion occurs only when men cut all the trees down, or plow up all the grass and weeds that would ab-

sorb the water and slow its rush. Exceptions are
cases where freaks of nature allow the earth to be
split or denuded, thus giving wind and rain oppor-
tunity to tear at the soil.

Here was such a case. Water had apparently be-
gun to trickle down an animal burrow near the top
of the hill—a badger, groundhog or prairie-dog hole.
Over a period of time, perhaps years, the water had
probed downward, as water does, ever gurgling and
searching for a lower level, until it had found an
ancient waterway beneath the hill and had pursued
it persistently to wash soft earth out of the clay
until there was an underground tunnel to the river.
Then, suddenly, the surface of the earth had
dropped of its own weight into the tunnel to create
a gash, open to the elements. It had eventually become an open sore on the hillside, inviting more
erosion. Along the great fissure, roots of trees were
bared, clinging desperately to the mixed soil of
yellow clay and dark humus exposed by the wound.
Smaller trees had already died and fallen into the
crevasse, which was thirty feet deep in places.

Sliding down into the ravine, I walked along its
bottom carefully, searching for rocks or bones of
another era. What I found was a small piece of coal,
embedded casually in a layer of clay ten feet below
the dark topsoil. This, then, was what my good buddy, Barney Heffner, might have died for—a piece of
coal. *A piece of coal?* What about a lot of coal? Supposing that the little lump of coal were only evidence of a vein of coal—a vein running under the
hill for perhaps miles along the river. Supposing
that Barney knew about the coal and had some
cockeyed plan to acquire the mineral rights to the
park, even to adjoining private property! Supposing

further that somebody else knew about the coal and wanted it—wanted it enough to kill for it. Well, that was a lot of supposing, but it was all I had for the moment and I latched onto it.

Climbing out of the gully, I tossed the coal aside, and began my ascent to the park, grasping at saplings to help myself up the hill. Coming out of the timber through a growth of sunflowers, I heard the sharp snap of a rifle bullet overhead and instinctively fell flat among weeds and brush, then crawled into the protection of a fallen log, just as the sound of the shot reached me. For an old infantry soldier, it was easy to identify the sound as that of a high-powered rifle, probably a nine millimeter Mauser or an old Springfield thirty-oh-six—something like that, although I am not expert enough to name the make and caliber of a rifle just from the sound of it. Certainly the projectile that had zipped past my head was fired from a flat trajectory weapon of some velocity. Nothing else cracks the air like that. There was no way of knowing where the shot came from, although to judge from the time lapse between the crack of the bullet as it passed and the sound of the explosion, it must have been some distance—a distant hilltop along the river, or even from a point on the mesa across the river. It could not have come from the park. That was only a hundred yards away. The two sounds would have come at almost the same instant.

After a few minutes of uneasy silence I slid backward, and suddenly leaping to my feet, ran like a scared jackrabbit downhill toward the sheltering forest. In heavy cover, I was a match for a rifleman at short range, and he couldn't see me from a distance. Treading carefully on the mushy floor, I made my way around the hill toward town, ever alert for the gunman, and hoping against hope that I'd run into him, face to face. It was eerie in the dark forest, alone on a day that was nearly night. Once a great white owl, disturbed by my presence leaped out of a towering linden tree to glide away on silent wings, and a lone crow flew high above the trees calling *haw-haw-haw*, looking for some friends.

Although a thousand people were going about their business a mile away, and automobiles were speeding up and down the highway within a half mile of me, it was easy to imagine that I was back in the nineteenth-century wilderness, sneaking through the woods after wild game for the table. It was almost a disappointment to come out of the trees and onto the street near the Heffner place. Their car was back, and Frankie was washing it, using a garden hose and sponge. Smoke wafted up from the chimney of the house, to fade quickly into a graying sky.

"Why don't you use warm water?" I asked. "You could freeze your mitts with that cold water."

"Warm water might crack the windows on a day like this. I'm just giving her a quick dousing to get the mud off." He squirted a thin stream against the car, pressing a thumb on one end of the hose to get pressure. Water splashed against glass and metal, to run down to the ground in sheets.

"Anybody come down from the park lately?" I asked.

The boy took his thumb off the hose and looked at me with some curiosity showing in his face. "Only the sheriff. Why?"

"Because somebody took a shot at me up there."

He didn't believe it. "Are you kidding?"

"Not at all. Why would I joke about a thing like that?"

"I don't know," he admitted, walking over to the house to turn off the hose. "When did it happen?" He began to wind the hose around a circular frame that was bolted to the house.

"Ten minutes ago," I replied. "When did Hohenstein come down? What was he doing up there?"

He shrugged. "I don't know, maybe a half hour ago. The sheriff goes up there all the time, to look out over his kingdom, I suppose. Do you think he shot at you?"

"Oh, no," I said hastily. "He was gone by the time the shot was fired. Besides, the shot didn't come from up there."

He asked me how I knew that, and I explained the whole thing to him. But I didn't say anything about the coal. It was going to be my own little secret for a while yet.

"Maybe it was an accident, Mr. Oberstdorf. It could have been somebody up on the mesa, shooting down at the river. Maybe some smart aleck shooting at a crow."

"Not likely, Frank. There wouldn't be any reason for a hunter over there to shoot at something over here, unless it was me. And then it wouldn't be an accident."

Right here, maybe I should clarify the difference between West River rifles and East River rifles. To begin with, you know by now that West River is an area of great distances and sparse vegetation and population. You can see an antelope or a deer a mile away, and he can see you. So, if you want to kill an animal, you need a high-velocity rifle with a tele-scopic lens. If you miss the shot, there probably won't be anybody around to get hit. In East River the farms are smaller, the vegetation heavy and ranges short. It is possible to get closer to your deer in a cornfield or in a forested creek bottom, so a less powerful firearm is required. In fact, the law regu-lates the kinds of weapons that may be used in given areas. In our county, east of the river, you are allowed to use bows and arrows, shotguns, or low-velocity rifles—like a thirty-five special or a thirty-thirty. Anybody caught east of the Deerhorn River with a high voltage piece is begging for trouble with the game commission. If all this seems unnecessari-ly drawn out, it is only that I am trying to establish that the shot was meant for me, without a doubt.

It gives you the creeps to know that somebody is out to kill you. It is unnerving to know that some-one you cannot identify is watching you, ready to strike at any time. I had that feeling at times, out in the jungle during the big war. Walking guard duty or moving through the forest on patrol, you never knew when a Jap sniper might be zeroed in on your head or your back, ready to squeeze the trigger of his little killing machine. More than one of our guys got nailed by a sniper hung up high in a tree, wait-ing for a shot. It is a weird feeling, walking around in good health, expecting to get it anytime.

To say that I wasn't scared would be a big, fat lie. Sure, you see this kind of thing in the movies, where the hero has been threatened or shot at or beaten up and he doesn't pay any attention to it but just goes right on doing stupid, brave things. Well, that is make-believe. When somebody shoots at you, it makes your toenails curl, unless you are a complete idiot. The more you think about it, the more you appreciate what a few grams of metal driven at nearly three thousand feet per second will do to your head or body when it smashes home. That is precisely why so many heroes are something less than intellectual marvels. If you haven't got brains enough to think about it, you don't get so scared. You show me a soldier who thinks a lot, and I'll show you one who does not have a load of medals on his tunic.

**4**

GOING TO WORK on Monday was a petty annoyance, because there was so much that I wanted to do on the Heffner case. For a long time I just sat looking out my office window at the square. The war-memorial statue and Twelfth Street were on my side of the building, and windows of the dime store and Wagner's Clothing Shop were still lighted up. The Corn Bowl bowling alleys and the Riviera Theater were dark. The theater is dark most of the time, now that all the kids are glued to television on Saturday and Sunday. There is a drive-in at Neu Koblenz, our big shopping center in Deerhorn County to the east. Teenagers like to go there, to watch rock musicals, eat popcorn, and feel each other up. But our little movie house, like so many throughout the country, is virtually out of business, open on occasion to show some of the blockbusters like *Jaws* and *Rocky*, but otherwise silent and dark.

If you are familiar with small towns, you know how the courthouse square is laid out, with the building sitting like some medieval castle on a square of ground, surrounded by rows of business houses. The courthouse is usually sandstone or limestone, quarried locally to save money. It houses all the county offices, from the sheriff to the super-intendent of schools, and is the cultural, legal and

social center of the county. Wide sidewalks lead
from each corner of the square, up to the building.
In most cases, there is a bandstand on one side of
the square and a war-memorial statue on the other
side. The statue is either a foot soldier with rifle at
port, or a horseman with drawn saber. Attached to
the base of the statue is a bronze plate containing
the names of all men of the county who have served
in our various wars. My name is on the one in Hessberg, as is that of my father. My grandfather's name
is not there, but may be on the one in Bregenz,
Vorarlberg, if they have one, and I'll bet that they
do.

My steam radiator was hissing like mad, heating
the room to tropical heights, so I turned a valve to
shut off the heat, then opened my window a crack
and began to sniff the disenchanting odors of the
Emhoff feedlots. This is one of the many charms of
living in a place like Hessberg, where the economy
is so beholden to enterprises that stink. When the
wind is wrong, you enjoy the mushy droppings of
thousands of cattle or the equally delightful odors
of the Union Rendering Works, down Boneyard
Creek. But then you can't have everything. One
must take the bitter with the better.

Our office opens officially at eight. At ten after,
Sara buzzed me to let me know that Ruby Wolf was
in the outer office. I told her to send Ruby right in
and she did. Ruby, who is fat even when she's not
pregnant, must have bruised herself on the door
frame coming in, she is that wide. When Ruby is
pregnant she is grossly obese, to use a medical term.
She was huffing and puffing like some old woman,
when to tell the truth, she is only thirty-five years
old.

Plumping down into the heavy armchair in front of my desk, she wheezed for a few seconds until she got enough wind back to say, "Hello, Obie. Think it will snow?"

"If it doesn't," I replied, "it will be a long, dry winter. What can I do for you, Ruby?"

She looked at me directly—proud but not afraid to ask for help. "Well, I hate to ask you, Obie, but we need help. Charlie has been out of work for a month, and we need groceries and coal. We are cold and hungry, and the light company is going to shut off our electricity if we don't pay our bill. As you can see, I am expecting again."

"Expecting what?" I asked, playing dumb.

She giggled. "You know what—look at me. When I get this fat, you know what I'm expecting!"

"A little bundle from heaven?"

She laughed at me. "My little bundles from heaven usually turn out to be little devils."

"That's not true," I told her. "You have some very nice, well-behaved children—they always call me Mr. Oberstdorf."

The fat lady looked pleased at that, and well she might, for it was true.

"What happened to Charlie's job at the feedlot?" I asked.

"Why," she replied, looking surprised, "didn't you know? Charlie got a double hernia lifting a sack of feed. He's been off work a month."

"Isn't Emhoff paying his salary?"

She sneered. "Are you kidding—that old miser? No, he had his foreman get my husband to sign a paper absolving the company of all blame."

"That's not legal," I advised her. "It won't stand up in court."

"They gave him two weeks' pay and told him not to come back. We're at rock bottom, Obie. We haven't had anything to eat for three days but cornmeal and skimmed milk."

"Why didn't you come sooner?" I demanded.

"Charlie wouldn't let me. You know how he is—stubborn and proud. We kept hoping that some miracle would happen so we wouldn't have to ask for help."

"Who is his doctor?"

"Olson."

"What is he doing for Charlie?"

Letting out a great sigh that shook her entire body, she said, "Nothing at all except trying to get him to go into the hospital for an operation."

"And?"

"Where would we get the money for an operation?" Staring at me dumbly, Ruby began to blubber, screwing her face into a frightful mask.

Getting up, I handed her a Kleenex and went out to the reception office, where Sara was reading the morning paper. The two secretaries, who were gossiping and sipping coffee when I showed up, quit talking and began to do busy things, opening up desk drawers, shuffling papers and uncovering their typewriters.

"Make out a grocery order for fifty dollars," I told Sara.

She laid her newspaper down on the back of her desk. "To Ruby Wolf?"

"No, to Charlie Wolf. Let *him* be the one to tolerate the indignity. Why should the wife always have to be the goat?"

Glancing into Louis Post's office, I saw that he was there, and I walked in to talk with him before he had a chance to slip away. He is a cagey young gentleman, always careful to keep a low profile for fear that I might have some work for him. He covers the West River region, which has three-fourths the area of our county and one-fourth the population, so he does a lot of traveling. Fanny Brodus, who shares his office, works rural East River, while I take the town. If you have been following me, you know that Fanny has half the entire case load, but don't get protective—Louis drives three times as many miles as she does, and I, being the director, have other duties, as you have seen. So, although Fanny has twice as many clients as we do, the actual work is pretty evenly divided. It must be admitted, however, that most of my business is walk-in, and that Sara, the best caseworker in our office, does a lot of my work for me.

Smiling evilly, Louis Post said, "Good morning, Mr. Oberstdorf. How goes the manhunt?" He is an outsider, a smart-aleck punk from Winnebago City who thinks that his M.S.W. makes him a great social worker. The truth is that he won't ever be a real social worker, if he stays on the job ten thousand years. He lacks the two basic qualities—humility and compassion. I intend to get rid of him as soon as possible, but I need something heavy, because we hire and fire under a state merit system. The merit system is like civil service in that it is virtually impossible to fire an incompetent or nasty employee. If I were like some department heads, I could just make his life so miserable that he would be glad to quit, but I don't have that kind of talent. So long as a person is halfway doing a job for me, I treat him the way I'd want him to treat me. That is one of my basic personality defects—I try hard to live by the golden rule. I don't always do it, but I try. It is a distinct disadvantage when dealing with people like Louis Post.

"Listen," I said, "how would you like to do me a favor?"

"Name it. You're the boss." He zipped his attaché case up and stuck his arms into a corduroy storm coat that had a big, mouton collar on it.

"Keep your ears open for any scuttlebutt on Barney Heffner. You know—any possible enemies, quarrels, business deals—anything that could be a clue. He was killed in your territory, and folks out there have a way of knowing things about each other."

"Gotcha, chief," he said facetiously, jamming a fur cap onto his peanut head, hamming it up, trying to sound like Don Adams.

Following him out to the front desk, I picked up the Wolf grocery order and returned to my office, where Ruby was waiting nervously. Giving the chit to her, I said, "Here is a grocery order for fifty dollars. It's in Charlie's name."

"He won't like that," she said slowly. "He'll have to go to the store."

"Would he rather let his family go hungry? He is the man of the family, and he should assume the burdens along with the joys."

"What joys?" she asked dully.

I almost said making babies, but didn't. There are certain things that are beneath the dignity of a welfare director, even in a small county.

Looking grim, she rose to leave, and I let her out a door that leads directly to the outside corridor. Halfway down the hall, she turned to call softly, "Thanks a lot, Obie."

"You're welcome," I assured her. "You tell Charlie to get his backside up here. You folks are going to need more help."

After telling my secretary that I was going out for a while, I walked down to the ground floor to the county clerk's office, where there is a plat of the county that shows ownership of all land. On page 14 I found the town plat, and running a finger up Ninth Street to its northern end, squinted to see what was there. The park was marked City Park, and below that in brackets and smaller letters, in India ink, U.S.A.

Well, I'll be doggoned, I thought, Old Man Miller sure goofed about that Moravian church thing.

But the county clerk, Helga Heber, restored my faith. "Oh, yes, the Moravians had that hill on a kind of lease for about five years, back in the nineties, then they moved out and the government leased it to the town for ninety-nine years at one dollar a year, with the stipulation that it would remain a park. It includes the entire hill—some eighty acres."

"Was there a church on the hill?"

"Of course." She seemed surprised that I didn't know but then she is a past president of the Kornfeld County Historical Society, so should know more than I do about such things. There was really no point in her being so uppity. Helga continued, "When the Cedar Ridge Indians were confined to their present reservation, in 1899, the Moravians closed their mission and abandoned the church. Over a period of time, people in the neighborhood tore it down and burned it in their stoves." She paused then. "If you are interested in the old building, Obie, there is a charcoal drawing of it upstairs in our club room."

I said, "No thanks," and went back up to the second floor to my lair, feeling pretty good about the whole thing. Thad Miller was not exactly right, but at the same time, was not exactly wrong. Nit-picking aside, the park was technically federal land, therefore subject to being filed on. All anybody had to do was put in his wooden stakes or stone markers and file a claim with the county clerk. Barney, unlike me, was a history buff. Doubtless, he had figured everything out and was preparing to file a mineral claim in the park. Unfortunately, somebody else was interested in the coal, and wanted the little truck driver out of the way. Now I had only to wait for somebody to file a mineral claim on the eighty acres and I'd have my killer. Or, conversely, I could file a claim and wait for somebody to assault me again. This, I decided, would be the best way to go, because the killer might take his own sweet time filing—maybe not file at all in view of current events. Or he might sit on the coal for a long time, so to speak, secure in the knowledge that nobody else knew about it. Yes, it would be best for me to file a claim and get the Heffner kid to file one for himself and his family. That way we would accomplish two things—flush the killer out into the open, and get ourselves a coal mine. You see how smug I was, how sure I was that my case was unraveling. However, smug as I was, I did not slacken my investigation, but instead kept sniffing like a coon hound on a hot trail. To bolster my coal mine theory, it was necessary to eliminate another possibility—that the act had been the work of a homicidal maniac from the state hospital. Also, amateur sleuth or not, I knew that there was always the chance that my conclusions were in error. So it was that I left my

trusty girl Friday in charge of the operation in my
office, and drove out to the hospital, presumably on
county business, but in fact to pick Bill Bridgeport's
brain. If anybody out there could help me, I knew,
it would be the chief of social service at Midwest.

To get there from town you follow Colfax out to
County Road 24 and turn north into rolling hills.
The hospital is two miles out on a gently tilted,
wooded hillside, facing the sun. The buildings are
drabby old piles of rock that blend into the hill on a
dull, winter day, seeming to be a natural part of the
landscape. Many of the buildings are empty, but
well kept, in keeping with state ownership. You
don't see any broken windows, weeds or tornado-
torn roofs on the buildings at our state hospital.
Even in an era of heavy inflation, maintenance is
cheap. The administrator simply hires a retired
craftsman from one of the small towns around to
supervise a repair job, and assigns a few patients to
do the work for him. Sometimes the craftsman did
not have to be brought in from outside. As one
might guess, there is a fair share of skilled blue-
collar workers in any state hospital, along with the
others. Even at Midwest, the catch basin for a large-
ly rural area, we have our share of painters, carpen-
ters, glaziers and roofers. So the buildings, although
not fully utilized, are in good condition. And there
is a nice tennis court, as well as a manicured ball
field behind the administration building, where I
usually park. On top of the ridge, there is a set of
sparkling, white farm buildings, sitting on the south
edge of a square mile of meadow and timber that
was once a fine grain and livestock operation. Now
it is no longer farmed, and is closed to hunting,
making it an unofficial game preserve, where every

species of bird and animal native to our region can be seen from time to time.

The way it was in the early days of the institution, people and public agencies still grew much of their own food. Most of the patients at the old insane asylum were rural people who knew how to garden, milk cows, and butcher hogs. Being committed to the asylum was not so much a change of life-style for them as merely a change of location. In custody they did most of the same things that they had done at home. There was a small cannery, a butcher shop and hen house, as well as a smoke house for curing meat. The farm kept a dairy herd and a few hogs. They farmed every inch of the section using horse-drawn equipment. Even today the barns at the farm are a treasure house of horse-drawn machinery, stored and never used again when the farm operation halted in the late 'thirties. About that time farming became specialized. The horses went and tractors came, and the old-timers didn't know how to operate the modern vehicles, and wouldn't learn. As bookkeeping became more prevalent in public institutions in our state, a new governor saw in all clarity that the hospital farm was a losing concept. So, after an appropriate period of political hemming and hawing in the state legislature, the farms in our state insitutions were, in effect, abolished. Now the only farm program at Midwest is the dairy, which provides milk, cheese and butter for both our state hospitals. The other hospital has a chicken-house-egg industry that provides eggs for both places. In the dairy, six patients under supervision of a merit-system foreman care for a hundred Holstein cows. Under another merit-system foreman, other patients process the milk in a modern milk house. The milk cows don't graze the farm, but eat commercial feeds brought in weekly on a big, sleek, sanitized truck. The feed is manufactured from all the best hay, grain, and vitamin supplements known to man.

When I went into the main building, Bill was downstairs in the cafeteria sipping tea with a couple of doctors. He has a horror of coffee, but drinks more caffeine in his tea than three other people drink in their coffee.

"Hello, there, Felix Oberstdorf," he cried, peering at me through heavy magnifying lenses that were held together by tortoiseshell frames. "How goes it with Sherlock Holmes, Junior?"

"Elementary, dear Bridgeport," I replied, "elementary."

Getting a cup of black coffee from an urn that sat just inside the entrance, I dropped a dime into a dish kept there for the purpose and went over to sit down.

"We're keeping a bed open for you," Bill said genially. "How's the wife?"

"Well, she's pretty good for an old lady, but she was better twenty years ago."

He grinned. "So were you. Who wasn't?"

The doctors, talking to each other, eyed me curiously and grunted some kind of barely intelligible greetings in keeping with our casual knowledge of each other. Doctors in state hospitals are strange birds, at least at Midwest. More than a few of them are former patients. Others are foreigners who don't speak English well enough to make a living in private practice.

The social worker and I kidded around until the doctors left, still absorbed in their little world, then I got down to business.

"Listen, Bill, have you got any homicidal maniacs here?"

"Only me." He studied my face closely and tipped his cup up to get the last drop of tea from it.

"I'm not kidding. You must have a few patients here who have killed people."

"Well, yeah, a couple—that we know about."

"Could I talk to them?"

Bill thought about it for a while before answering. "I guess so, Obie, but off the record. You have no official status in law enforcement, and I have none in granting interviews like this. Normally the official crime investigator would make a formal request of the administrator, and there would have to be a couple of doctors and recording secretaries on hand to protect the patients' civil rights." He seemed uncertain about getting involved.

"On the other hand," I told him, "if I should come out here to interview a patient on behalf of the welfare department in his own county, there would be no hassle about it."

He smiled broadly. "Oh, is that what you're doing? Why didn't you say so? You are so devious!"

"Is it possible," I asked, "that one of your homicidal patients could have been away from the hospital the day that Barney got it?"

"I doubt it. We keep pretty close tabs on them. We got burned three or four years ago when Ike Bauers ran away and went downtown. He went into a saloon and threatened a couple of sheepherders with a bar stool. Irv Glotz talked him out of it and brought him home. There was no harm done, but the administrator raised all kinds of hell with the staff about it."

"I'll bet he did," I said, visualizing the public

indignation of the Midwest superintendent, Dr.
Francis E. Wiggington III. The coffee break was
over and employees were leaving the room, filing
past a large dishpan where they deposited their
dirty cups.

"Let's take a hike up to maximum security,"
Bridgeport said, "where we keep all our desperate
criminals." He smiled thinly, indicating a disbelief
in the presence of killers in his bailiwick. Some
social workers are like that. They think that society
is the collective culprit, that nobody is ever individ-
ually guilty of any crime. I don't buy that. In my
book, there is no such thing as society, just a world
full of individual men and women. And some of
them are cold-blooded killers.

Walking out of the building and down a short
flight of steps to the sidewalk, Bill asked, "Are your
kids coming home for Christmas?"

"Heinie is. I don't know about Earl. He will if he
can get a hop into Win City or Omaha. There is a lot
of air traffic between S.A.C. and Frankfurt, but
Christmas is a bad time to mooch a ride." We
walked uphill on a wide strip of cement that led to
each rock pile in turn, and halfway up the hill he
led me into a small, two-story edifice that had steel
bars on its windows and doors. Pressing a button at
the front entrance, Bill waited patiently for a
response, all the while humming "Rock of Ages"
tonelessly.

Before long the door opened inward and a very
large young man, who looked like a Swede, stood
glowering at us.

"Hi, Pat," Bill said. "We came to see Bauers and
Washington. This is Felix Oberstdorf. Pat Van
Gerit."

"Glad to know you," the kid growled, not seeming glad at all. And almost in the same breath he yelled, "Washington! Bauers!" And he stomped upstairs heavily, calling out for the two homicidal maniacs at the top of his voice. At least I hoped it was the top of his voice. If he could holler any louder, I'd hate to hear it. In a few minutes he returned, hitting each step solidly with his big feet. Behind him came two men, one white, one black. They wore russet robes over gray cotton pajamas. Their feet were encased in sheepskin house slippers.

"Hi, Jeff." Bill grinned, reaching out a hand toward Washington, "I haven't seen you in a month. Don't you ever come down to recreational therapy anymore?"

"Not since I finished my picture, Mr. Bridgeport. Anyhow, I been sick for the past couple of weeks— my arthritis is acting up on me again."

"This is Mr. Oberstdorf from the welfare department, fellows," Bill told them jovially. "He would like to talk to you about Barney Heffner."

"Case closed," snapped Ike Bauers, an elder with cloudy eyes and gray whiskers. "I killed him."

This news startled me, but not Bridgeport, who continued to smile. "You killed George Custer, too, didn't you?"

"Right as rain, Billy," the old man croaked. "I was out on the creek that day, picking blueberries for my squaw."

"What creek?" I asked innocently.

Bauers looked at me crossly. "*What* creek? *What* creek? Why, the Little Big Horn Creek, you dummy. They always call it the Little Big Horn *River* in storybooks, but it ain't no river—just a little creek about twenty feet wide. That yellow-haired bastard was up there on the hill, shooting at my in-laws, and I just walked up to him and shot him dead with my old Kentucky long rifle.''

"That makes you about a hundred and twenty years old," I said.

He nodded. "You're close, mister. I'll be a hundred and seventeen years old, come Christmas.''

"Christmas?''

· He stared at me in disbelief. "Are you hard of hearing, or have you forgot that Jesus Christ was born on Christmas? Well, sir, I was fifteen years old when I went to live with the Crows, and eighteen when I married Carries Blanket. I had to fight the biggest goddamned warrior in Montana for her hand. The chief stripped us, tied our right hands together and gave us each a big knife. Lucky for me I was lefthanded. It runs in my family.''

"Ike killed Adolph Hitler, too,'' Bill said gravely.

"Who told you that? I didn't tell you that, Billy.''

"One of your girl friends told me—Freda Fenske.''

Ike scowled. "That little bitch! She promised not to tell anybody. Even the Argentine F.B.I. never knew who did it.''

"Listen, you crazy old dingbat," the orderly said, "you haven't been out of this building in a month.''

"*Who's* crazy?'' the patient demanded. "*You're* the crazy one, Patrick. I go out every night.''

Pat stared at him, goggle-eyed. "How the hell do you go out, with the doors and windows barred?''

"My spirit goes, you big clown—right through the walls. Hell, I'm in Win City nearly every night, getting stewed, screwed and tattooed!''

The young orderly was astounded. Shaking his

head from side to side, he told us, "Boy, this is a home for weirdos, but that old man takes the cake." Gazing at Ike Bauers, he said: "Boy, you really take the brass-bound pee pot!"

Ike stared back at Pat. "Don't beat around the bush, Patrick. If you think I'm telling lies, just say so."

"Oh, God!" the kid said helplessly, rolling his eyes upward.

The black fellow, a smiling man of forty-five or fifty years, went over to the far wall of the room and began rocking in an easy chair. He moved back and forth from the hips rhythmically, crooning a dirge.

"Another week," Van Gerit complained, "and I'll be as wacky as they are."

As we started for the front door, Bauers followed, sidling obliquely like a fiddler crab in the sand, crying, "Mr. Oberstdorf, don't you want to hear how I killed Attila the Hun?"

Outside, huddling against a rising north wind, I asked Bill whether Ike had ever killed anybody, and he told me the story.

"He was always weird, but I doubt that he really killed anybody. In 1934 Ike's old man was found dead in the barn, with his head caved in, after a family quarrel. A passing hobo might have killed him for what little money he had in his pocket. Or one of his mules might have kicked him in the head. Nobody knows for sure, but the family saw a chance to get rid of Ike. He was strange—a constant source of embarrassment to them. So, they used the death of his father as an excuse to commit Ike. He's better off here, for that matter. People in his home county were cruel to him."

"Where is he from?"

"Deerhorn County, south of Blue Springs a few miles. His family is long gone. His mother died and his sibs moved away."

"It's a damn shame that a person can be salted away on a funny farm for life, just on the say-so of embarrassed relatives."

"Yes, it is," the social worker agreed, "but it's not that easy anymore, as you know. Ike was sent up more than forty years ago."

"How old is he?"

"I'm not sure, maybe seventy-five or so, maybe more. Are you serious about Barney's death being a murder, Felix?"

"Of course I'm serious. We found his dog dead, shot through the head and tossed into a ravine. Do you think that Barney killed Shaky, buried the rifle, then shot himself in the belly?"

"Maybe some irate husband or boyfriend shot him," Bill suggested, as we neared the administration building. "He was quite a cocksman."

I stopped in my tracks, stunned. "Who told you that? I've never heard that before. What makes you think that Barney was that kind of person?"

"What makes me think it," he replied, gazing at me levelly, "is that a dozen or more of our female patients have told us that over a period of years, and they can't *all* be liars. It's like this, Obie. Some of them may lie some of the time, and all of them may lie some of the time, but they don't all lie all of the time."

Leaving him at the entrance to his building, I thanked the social worker for his help, then went around the place toward my car, thinking hard. How typical! You look for one thing and find another. I had drawn a blank on the patients, but learned something about my dead friend that I had never known—never suspected.

On my way back to the office I continued to mull it over, and had to admit that it made sense. After all, Barney's male friends had loved him and would have done anything for him—why not his female friends as well? But then, I was loath to admit to myself that he might have taken advantage of mentally ill women. But maybe he didn't. Maybe he knew them *before* they were hospitalized. In that event, one could not fault him so badly. If every man in Kornfeld County admired Barney Heffner, why not all the women? True, he was not a handsome man. However, Casanova, Cellini and Cyrano were not handsome men either, but they got their share. Maybe the ladies threw themselves at him.

It was at this point that my coal-mine theory began to waver a bit, but not much, for I am a plodding man. Once I get an idea into my head, right or wrong, I do not readily disabuse myself of it. Some people regard this as a Germanic trait. They call it Dutch stubbornness, which it is not. It's a personal thing, having nothing whatsoever to do with national origin. Nevertheless, it bothered me all the way to my office where Charlie Wolf waited for me, having been admitted to my inner sanctum by Sara.

"With his hernia," she explained, "I thought it might be more comfortable for him in your office, on a softer chair."

Charlie was doing the Australian crawl in self-pity. "This is the hardest thing I ever had to do in my life, Felix."

"You're not dead, yet," I said.

"I'd just as well be. Any man who can't support his family is better off dead!"

"Who is going to take care of them, then?"

He rubbed his nose with the back of one horny hand. "Hell, I didn't think about that. But Jesus Christ, man, what am I going to do?"

"For one thing, you can knock off the self-pity and self-incrimination and start making plans to get that hernia repaired."

"Great. Let's look around for a doctor who works for nothing, and a hospital that gives away beds." He sounded bitter.

"Just simmer down and listen to me," I suggested. "First of all, I'm going to take your application for Aid To The Disabled. Then I'm going to take your wife's application for Aid To The Families Of Dependent Children."

"Oh, my God—disabled—dependent children—all that damn charity!"

"Then," I continued, "I am going to call the light company and guarantee payment of your light bill. Next, I am going to ask the mayor to send over a load of wood for your stove. They cut trees the year round and stockpile it. You had as well get some of it."

"What did I ever do?" He wailed.

"Listen here," I told the man, "you are getting to be a big pain in the butt! I am doing my best to help you, and all you can do is wail and moan like a bull with its balls caught on a picket fence! Jesus Christ, there is no such thing as charity anymore. We're all in this world together. You show me somebody who is not on some kind of federal, state or county hand-out, and I'll show you somebody who has not been born yet. Look at all the doggone farmers getting paid for not growing crops, all the loafers drawing unemployment compensation, all the grad students goofing off on federal grants. Anybody who works for any public agency is accepting charity. A lot of guys in this town are getting disability compensation from the V.A. I'm one of them. Do I look disabled to you?'' I didn't tell him that I carry three or four pieces of shrapnel in my legs.

Charlie then confided that he was getting ten percent disability compensation from the Veterans' Administration. It was apparent that he was feeling better all the time.

''When you leave here,'' I told him, ''you go over to see Ed Meister at the County Veterans' Service office and tell him that you need some help. He should give you a hundred right off the top of the deck.

''Another thing,'' I told him. ''You get your ass over to the Neu Koblenz office of the Vocational Rehabilitation office and tell Albert Johnson over there I sent you—he's the district supervisor. Tell him that I sent you over there to get your hernia repaired so you become a tax *payer* instead of a tax *user*.'' The cliché nearly gagged me.

''Thanks,'' he said. ''By the way, are you having any luck on the Heffner case?''

Shrugging, pursing my lips, I told him that it was very slow going without any solid evidence to study, but that I had a few leads and was following them when I could find time.

''I hope you find the guy who killed him, Felix. Old Barn was quite a man. We was in the service together, you know.'' Charlie got up to go, and standing, he gave the appearance of great power, although he is only about six feet tall and one eighty-five. "Yeah," he said. "We had some great times down at Fort Leonard Wood, Missouri. Boy, he was *some* lady's man!"

My ears pricked up. "What did you say?"

"I said he was some lady's man. Why?"

"Because it has a familiar ring. I heard the same thing from somebody else about thirty minutes ago, only in slightly different language."

Charlie grinned: "Oh, yeah? What kind of language?"

"Well, let's see now. It seems to me that the word was something like *cocksman*."

"That's what he was," Wolf said. "Man, I could tell you some stories that would rattle your spurs, Felix! No doubt some guy caught old Barney in the wrong bed and let him have it."

"He wasn't shot in bed," I said. "He was shot way out in the boondocks."

"I was speaking figuratively," he replied, and reached for the doorknob.

"Charlie!"

He hesitated in the doorway. "Yeah?"

"I'll be over in the morning with the papers for you and Ruby to sign."

**5**

A LONG TIME AGO in Hessberg, there was a family by the name of Black Coyote. John Black Coyote was an independent man who did not like reservation life, perhaps for some of the same reasons that I did not like army life when I was in. The difference was that I had to stay and he didn't. He brought his family to town, and they stayed three or four years during the Depression era. He had a team of roan horses, a weather-beaten wagon and a rusty plow. These were his principal tools of livelihood. With the team and wagon, he hauled junk, groceries and furniture around our little town. In the spring he plowed gardens, and in the winter he plowed snow, clearing alleys and driveways for people. His snow-plow consisted of some heavy planks bolted together and reinforced by a length of V-Frame that he screwed to the front edge. As he was a large, gentle man, afraid of nobody, John was sometimes called upon to serve as a deputy sheriff or assistant town marshal. These jobs were infrequent and much sought after at a time when so many people were in need, so it wasn't a major source of income for the family. He received a brown envelope from Kansas City once each month, which according to our long-time postmaster, Allen Zabriskie, was a government check. As it was from an office of disbursement,

nobody ever knew what it was for, whether from
the Bureau of Indian Affairs or from the Veterans'
Administration. We did know that like many Cedar
Ridge Indians, John had served with distinction in
World War I. We knew this because some of our
local veterans belonged to the legion post in Neu
Koblenz, along with veterans from Cedar Ridge. In
that day, the legion post at Neu was the only one in
our region. After the big war, the one that I was in,
every town in every county had its own legion post,
and most of them had V.F.W. posts. But that is
another story.

Sometime around 1935, John, his wife and their
six children disappeared overnight. They loaded all
their possessions into the wagon and took off for
parts unknown. Al Zabriskie didn't even know
where they went, because John had not given him a
change-of-address notice. But the brown envelope
did not come from Kansas City anymore, so we assumed that the big Indian had sent his change-of-
address letter to the office in Kansas City. I don't
know why they left, and don't really care, because
in fifty years I have seen hundreds of people come
and go. And there wasn't anything different about
the Black Coyote family except Susan. They were
very much like a lot of poor families in Kornfeld
County, white and Indian. But Susan who was my
age, happened to be different from all the others. In
appearance, she was much like other little half-
Indian girls, or even like many little German girls in
the county.

What made Susan different was a strange kind of
dynamism, not love, not sex, but a strong, compell-
ing attraction. At age ten, boys and girls do not normally feel the sex urge, and we were not exceptions,

but Ace Harmsen and I used to sit in a bower of lilac
bushes along Boneyard Creek with Susan, pressed
against her tightly, holding her hands, kissing her
hair and cheeks, with no thought of love or sex. She
would sit quietly between us, making no effort to
return our ardor, as we thrilled to the touch of her
soft body between us. It was a sweet, innocent
childhood experience, one that I never really knew
again, although Milly Heffner reminds me a great
deal of Susan Black Coyote. She has the same great
gray eyes, soft auburn hair and jersey cream skin.
But more than that there is an aura of mystery, an
indefinable dynamism about her that compels me to
enjoy her presence, as I have not enjoyed a presence since Susan left town almost a half century
ago. I have even had the crazy notion that by some
chance, Milly could be Susan's daughter. That, of
course, is pure nonsense. She is the third daughter
of Klaus and Anna Borchers.

Ace didn't come home after the war. He met a
belle in South Carolina, and went there to live after
the service. When he came back for the town cen-
tennial a few years ago, I made it a point to introduce
him to Milly and ask him whether she reminded him
of anybody. Without hesitation he said, "Sure—
Susan Black Coyote."

So this may give you some idea as to how I felt
about Milly, and why I didn't waste any time getting over there on Tuesday afternoon, right after
lunch when Sara told me that Milly had called and
wanted to see me. When I got there it was one-
thirty and the kids were in school, except Frankie,
who was out at his grandfather's place feeding cattle.

Milly looked better than she had looked immedi-

ately after the funeral, as one might expect. She
had probably been able to get some sleep, and to
have her hair done at her favorite place in Neu. But
she was still in mourning, as evidenced by the black
jersey sheath that clothed her body from neck to
ankles, just loose enough to be respectable.

She greeted me warmly. "Thanks for coming,
Felix. Would you care for a drink?"

"Well, I was in the neighborhood, anyway," I
told her, "to see Thad Miller. Yes, make it a lemon
sour with whiskey, if you please."

After bringing our drinks from the kitchen, she
curled up on one end of a long, leather couch, drawing her slippered feet up under the jersey skirt. She
sat, staring absently for a time, seeming to think
about what she was going to say, and while she was
doing that, I was undressing her mentally, at the
same time feeling like a dirty old man. For, after all,
she was the recent widow of a dear friend, and I
was almost old enough to be her father.

Finally she spoke, turning the clear, gray eyes full
upon me. "I need your advice about something,
Felix."

"Anything I can do, Milly, now or later. I want
you to know that you will always have a friend in
me. Barney Heffner was one of the finest men I
ever knew. You can ask me to do anything that you
would ask him to do." If that sounds suggestive, it
was not, because I was not talking about that. I was
talking mundane chores that a husband normally
does—counseling the kids, moving the furniture,
hiring a lawyer, for instance.

"Thanks a lot," she said. "I really appreciate
that, Felix." She paused momentarily to take a sip
of her drink, then went on. "Obie, you probably

know that Barney had this thing about Albert Schweitzer.''

"Yes, Frankie told me all about it the other day.''

"You know that Barney wanted to put a statue of Schweitzer in the town square.''

"Yes.''

"Well, what do you think of it?''

"Why not? If you feel that you can afford it, hire an artist and get permission from the town council to set up a statue on the courthouse lawn. There is plenty of room on the west side of the building.''

"They turned him down once,'' she reminded me.

"Yes, but that was before he was killed. Now he is a kind of local hero. A memorial to Schweitzer would be about the same thing as a memorial to Barney.''

She wasn't yet convinced. "Wouldn't it cost a great deal of money? We can't spend more than a couple of thousand dollars of the insurance money. Dad would spend as much as necessary, but the kids and I want this to be our own gift to the memory of Barney, doing something that he really wanted done.'' She took another drink and waited for my response to that. It was almost as if she thought that I was a part-time expert on courthouse statues.

"I don't really know,'' I admitted, "but I'm going to be in Win City this week, girl. If you want me to, I'll check it out—find a good sculptor and get his price. If you can't get a statue for two thousand, maybe you can settle for a big chunk of granite with a brass plate on it. The metal plate might have a bas-relief head of Schweitzer on it, with a narrative beneath telling about his life, as well as a few words about the donor.''

She was mildly enthusiastic. "That sounds good

to me. There must be several good sculptors in Winnebago City.''

"If not," I replied, "we can try Omaha, or even
shoot the works and go to Kansas City.''

She sighed in relief. "I knew I could count on you,
Obie. You are so dependable—so comforting.''

On that note, I bailed out. When a good-looking
woman finds a man dependable and comforting, it
begins to get sticky. My glass was empty and I didn't
want another. I don't like to drink when I'm working, and I rarely do it.

As I approached her front door, Milly stopped me.
"Obie.''

"Yeah?''

"What about this murder investigation? What
kind of luck are you having?''

"Not much. Why? Do you have some ideas?''

"Well, I do have *one* idea—I wish you'd drop it.''

"*Drop* it?'' I stared at her in disbelief. "Mildred,
there is a killer at large. He has to be caught and
punished!''

"It's upsetting the girls,'' she replied sullenly.
"All the kids at school are joking about it.''

"Let them joke,'' I said. "It's not a kid's game.
This is serious, grown-up business.''

"You said that you would do *anything* for me,''
she reminded me.

"Yes, I did, but that does not include copping out
on a promise that I made to myself and Barney. I'm
going to get that murdering animal if it's the last
thing I ever do!''

When I went outside, I saw Thad in his yard, put-
tering around, and getting into my car, I backed
diagonally across the street to his lot.

Looking up from his repair job on the fence, he
grunted.

"I see you got yourself a little nooky, kid."

"What do you mean by that, you old goat?"

"Wasn't you just across the street, or was that your twin brother?" he demanded.

"You are an evil old man, Thad. Your mind is always in the gutter."

"You'll get your tit in a wringer fooling around with that little squaw," he warned me. "She is bad medicine."

"Why don't you let *me* worry about that, and you worry about getting cleaned up? Your doggone overalls could stand alone. Mr. Miller, you would stink a skunk off a gut wagon!"

Unperturbed, he continued to work on the fence, using a rusty pair of pliers that might have been as old as he was. Twisting at the wire, he asked, "Why don't you come up with something new, Oberstdorf? The first time I heard that one was in 1884—I was just a kid then."

"You, my friend, were just a kid in 1784."

Choosing to ignore that, he asked me when I was going to pick up the bell, and I said maybe later in the day if I could get Frank Heffner to haul it for me in his truck. Then I gave him the bottle of Ohio wine that I had brought him, and warned him not to drink it all at once.

"This is my favorite wine—sauterne," he told me after a long pull at the bottle. "I like dry wine."

"Hell, you like *any* kind of wine, you old fraud," I told him.

"That's not nice," he complained, looking hurt. "Just for that, I may not tell you what I forgot to tell you the other day."

"What's that?"

"I'm not saying."

"Who brought you the wine?"

He sniffed importantly, squinting in the sunlight, and brought out a pair of greasy binoculars that had been concealed under the bib of his overalls. The glasses were tied to a soiled cord that went around his neck. His neck was soiled, too, with the wrinkles showing as black lines.

"I see everything that goes on around here," he boasted, lifting the bottle for another snort.

"Cut out the bull, Thad. What did you forget to tell me?"

"Don't rush me, kid. What did I forget to tell you? Oh, yes, I forgot to tell you that somebody was watching Barney's house."

"Who?"

The old man glared at me. "How the hell do I know *who*? It was just some dude in a black car. He used to park up on the hill and watch the house until Barney left. At first, I thought it was one of Milly's boyfriends, waiting for old Barn to leave, but it wasn't. The guy never stopped at the house. I think he followed Heffner sometimes. I watched him go up the street, and then come back down when Barney left."

I looked at Thad, pursed my lips, and knit my brows. "Too bad you didn't get his license number."

"I did."

"You did what?"

"I got his license number."

I was dumbfounded. "You got his license number?"

"That's what I said, Obie. What's the matter, are you hard of hearing or something? Or don't you understand English?"

With that kind of dialogue, little by little, I eventually got the story. Old Man Miller got incensed one day when the driver of the black car ran over a squirrel that was crossing Ninth Street. It so happened that the old boy was very fond of that specific squirrel and wanted to see justice done. So, he glassed the man's license number and wrote it down, then turned it over to Sheriff Hohenstein, who was in the habit of going up to the park almost every day.

"He snoops," Thad said of Hohenstein. "The big bastard goes up the hill all the time to spy on the town with a big spy glass. On the way down he stops to see Miz Heffner."

"What did he do about the man in the black car?"

Thad stared at me with his *disgusted* face. "*Do*? Hell, he didn't do nothing. Said there is no law against running over a squirrel."

I was curious about one thing more. "Did you tell Kurt that the man in the black car was watching Barney's house?"

"Nope, he didn't ask me and I didn't tell him. Why should I do his work for him when he won't even arrest a squirrel killer?"

"Where is the license number?"

Without answering, he motioned for me to follow him into his house, and because it took him so long to find the paper with the license number on it, I couldn't hold my breath and had to suck in a lungful of the foul air. It made me halfway sick.

Groping, fumbling, cursing, Thad eventually found a scrap of brown paper with the number on it—25H2964.

"That's Winnebago County," I said excitedly. "He is probably a hired killer from the city."

My elderly friend tried to shoot me down. "Maybe he wanted to stop in on little Miz Heffner, but didn't have the guts. But the sheriff stopped. He still does."

"He does?"

"Sure. Why not? Why give up a good thing just because dear Barney is dead?"

"You sure are full of answers," I told him. "How come you're not rich?"

"I was once. Maybe I'll tell you about it some time."

"I can hardly wait," I replied, as he jerked a dirty sheet off a portable television set that rested atop a packing crate in a corner of the hog-pen room.

Thad twisted a button to light up the tube, which began flickering with unstable, horizontal lines. As the sound rose and the picture came into focus his old head fell slowly forward onto his chest, and he began to snore loudly, causing the tobacco-stained hair of his beard to flutter.

Things were happening so fast that I was beginning to get confused. Within thirty minutes, I had been unofficially called off the case by the dead man's widow, and had been presented the license number of a car that might belong to her husband's killer. Also, I had learned that the lady might not have been so pure in fact as she was in my romantic mind. The evidence seemed to be there. Why would the sheriff have been visiting Barney's wife, if not to sip of Barney's wine? It's bad enough to fool around with a widow whose husband is barely cold. To fool around while that man is alive is worse. Some old-fashioned people call it adultery, a serious crime for a politician to become involved in.

My imagination, unstable at best, began to run wild. Could it be that Kurt and Milly were lovers and wanted to get rid of old Barney? If so, where did the black car fit in? Did Milly hire him to do Barney in? My God, what was I saying to myself? How could I even *think* such thoughts?

Leaving Thad's shack, closing the door carefully to prevent its being blown open, I stood for a minute, gazing across the street at a once-happy household now crumbling into uncertainty and disenchantment. Beyond the little house and its protective trees, I could see a gray blanket of snow clouds creeping down from the mesa, coming slowly toward town. Although the sun still shone on Hessberg, a wind had come up and it was getting colder by the minute.

There have been times in our part of the country when the temperature dropped forty degrees in an hour. We get fierce blizzards off the high plateau, and they don't give warning, but come rushing out of the northwest, driven by stinging, icy gales, to bury the valley in snow.

By the time I reached Colfax Avenue, there was no sun in sight and snow was blowing across the street in a mounting ground blizzard. If you don't know what a ground blizzard is, it is just that—snow driven laterally across the earth at gale force. It may rage over the land to a depth of ten or twelve feet or more, while above that level all is tranquil. We get these frequently in Hessberg, when snow is dumped onto us from the big table and caught in the sweep of high winds funneling down the Deerhorn Valley.

There was a purple and tan patrol car parked at the Westside Café, a big truck stop and lunch counter at Tenth and Colfax. It was, I guessed, Abner Collins, out from Neu Koblenz, so I pulled in for a visit and found him alone in a back booth, dunking a glazed doughnut in creamed coffee. His big hat lay beside him on the seat, giving everybody a chance to see that his golden curls did not cover all his head, but only a strip around it, leaving the top nearly bare. Abner is a beefy man in his late forties, an outlander, but a very nice man. He used to hunt the West River with Barney and me now and then, and you get to really know a man when you hunt with him. Some people are pure hogs on a hunting trip. They carry booze with them, point their rifles or shotguns at you, and stomp through the fields like wild elephants. Others, Abner included, are real gentlemen, who value your life as well as their own. They don't shoot birds from in front of your barrel, or point their guns carelessly, and don't drink while hunting. Alcohol on a hunting trip is really bad news—as bad as alcohol on a Sunday drive in the family sedan. But this is not to be an alcoholism lecture. Just let me say that an experienced hunter can give you a pretty good psychological evaluation of a hunting companion after two or three trips to the country.

"What's up, Felix?" The trooper greeted me genially. "I hear you're breaking into the private-eye business, partner."

"Call it that if you wish, Ab. I just don't happen to believe that old Barney would be careless enough to shoot himself going through a fence."

"I don't either, Felix, but what can you do about it? You are a social worker, not Sherlock Holmes or Sam Spade."

Glancing out at the gasoline pumps, now blurry in the storm, he muttered, "This damn storm is going to ruin my whole day! It will take me until six o'clock to work my way back to headquarters, and I'm off duty at five." Turning back to me, he said, "No kidding, Obie, you should let the police handle this."

I laughed at his earnest concern. "*What* police? Old Irv is out of the question, and Hohenstein is thoroughly incompetent, as you know. Besides that, I think he was fooling around with Barney's wife."

"Milly? That's hard for me to believe, Obie."

"Me, too, but there is strong indication that it's so." And I told him about Thad Miller, and about the man in the black car.

"Have you got that license number handy?"

Feeling a tinge of victory, I handed over the number. Pulling on his hat, Ab walked past the cash register where he dropped his check, along with the change to pay for his doughnut and coffee, then went to his cruiser to radio Neu Koblenz for the owner of the car. The operator there would contact the police department in Win City to get the information. I followed him.

"This amateur police work is dangerous," he scolded me. "Somebody could take a shot at you."

I laughed at that. "Your warning comes a bit late, Ab. It has already happened." I filled him in.

"Did you report it to the police?" he asked sternly.

"No. If I did, my wife would find out about it and pull me off the case. Besides that, it would be an exercise in futility, as you well know. Irv and Kurt are both entirely without resources to handle something like this. I'll find the killer myself."

"If he doesn't find you first."

"So be it," I said. "The Lord willing, we shall meet."

"What about the kid?" Ab asked. "What is his name—Fred? Is he in college? It seems to me that his grandfather wanted to help him go to school."

I gave Ab a searching look. "Boy, you are only about six months behind the times. *Frank* wanted to go into the service when he got out of high school His dad was in during Korea, and the kid wanted to follow in Barney's footsteps. The family wanted him to go to ag college."

"So?"

"So, they compromised. The boy enlisted in the Marine Corps Reserve and went to California for basic training. After basic, he elected to take a course in auto mechanics. He was gone five months altogether, and has been home since the first of the month—plans to start college next semester."

There was a buzz on the radio, and a businesslike, feminine voice from the patrol station. "Neu Koblenz calling Car Fifty-Two—come in, Sergeant Collins."

"Collins here, over."

"The license number you queried on belongs to a 1976 Plymouth Valiant, registered to Brian Keelan. He was paroled from the State Penal Complex three months ago after serving ten years on a murder charge. He has been known to carry firearms." She was silent, waiting to hear from Ab.

Collins, putting the little mike up to his face, obliged her. "Thanks, Kay. I'm coming in now. The storm is getting really bad out here, so I may not see you before you go home. See you tomorrow then."

Turning to me squarely, he said, "You heard it, Obie. The man is dangerous. You are playing with matches, buddy. This gink would rather kill a *dozen* social workers than return to stir!"

"Nobody else is interested," I replied, beginning to heat up. "What am I supposed to do, Abner? That clown, Hohenstein, won't do anything but grin and backslap. He's a lousy, small-time hack, just like O'Shay. They make a great team. One of my best friends get knocked off, and everybody shrugs it off as an accident. What would you do in my place?"

He had a firm and simple answer. "Why, I'd call the highway patrol, Felix. We are the state police department, with a very good and highly professional criminal investigation division. We are not just a bunch of motorized cowboys who chase speeders and deliver gasoline to stranded motorists."

As it was getting cold in the car, Ab started the motor, and after a couple of minutes, turned on the heater.

"Let's review this case," he suggested, getting ready to write in a spiral notebook with a yellow, ball-point pen. "First, a man is found dead on a barbed-wire fence, ten yards from a gate. His belly is blown open by a shotgun—presumably his own—which is lying nearby with one exploded shell in the chamber. Now, everybody except you and the dead man's son believes that the dead man killed himself accidentally, while going through the fence."

"The dead man," I reminded him, "was our good friend, Barney Heffner."

"Yes," he said, at the same time watching a stock truck run a red light at the corner of Tenth and Colfax. The vehicle turned into the station and pulled up to the gas island for service.

"Excuse me," Abner said, getting out of the car, "while I give that bastard a ticket."

The ticket writing took about two minutes, including all the head shaking and arm waving of the driver, who just happened to be my second cousin, Alfie Carlsen, from Dresden in the next county.

Returning, Ab complained, "These goddamned rich farmers give me a pain in the ass—think they can do any damned thing they want to. Where were we?"

"Barney is found dead, and everybody thinks he shot himself."

"Oh, yeah. Then you and the kid find Barney's little dog dead in a ravine nearby. There is a hole in his head—probably from a twenty-two bullet."

"Correct."

Writing swiftly, the patrolman pursued it. "Next, you are shot at in the park by a high-powered rifle. Finally, you learn that a man driving a black car had been seen several times prior to Barney's death watching the Heffner place. You get the license number of the car from an interested neighbor, and it turns out to be the car of a paroled convict."

"Right," I said. "You sure are handy with that pen and notebook, Sergeant. You'd make a great court reporter."

He chuckled. "How do you think I got started, Obie? Anything else before I light out for home?"

"No, I guess not—except that the sheriff of Kornfeld County was seen at the Heffner house a number of times, before the death of Mr. Heffner, and after, always when Mrs. Heffner was alone."

He looked at me closely. "Is that supposed to have some significance, Felix?"

I shrugged. "Maybe, maybe not. I'll leave that up to the experts in your office at Win City. After all, *they* are the professionals."

So far I was the only one who knew about the old

coal vein except Thad Miller, and I didn't intend to spill it before I had a chance to file claims for myself and the Heffner family. Besides, there was still a chance that the killer or his employer would file a claim. If so, I'd have them cold turkey.

"I'll send this report to the state office," Abner promised. "You should hear something from them in a few days. Meantime, for Christ's sake, Obie, watch your step."

I promised that I would watch my step, and he revved his motor as a signal that he was ready to head for home. So I got out of the car and stood in the swirling storm as he pulled out.

Well, so much for that. Feeling temporarily fulfilled by the turn of events, pleased that somebody in an official capacity was involved at last, I turned my thoughts to coal. It was my intention to file lode claims, for myself and the Heffners, in the park. Four claims would cover the entire hill, giving us all the coal therein. I planned to file claims for Frankie and Milly, as well as for Ellen and myself. There could be enough coal in the hill to change our lives for the better. On the other hand, it could be that there would be little or no coal under the great ridge. But all we could lose was the filing fees—less than a hundred dollars for all the claims, and it could be very beneficial not only for us, but for the entire town. Because if that hill harbored coal, nearby hills probably held some, too. If so, we might revive the mining industry in Hessberg.

Automobiles and trucks moved slowly along Colfax, probing the rushing sheet of snow with thin beams of head lamps, grinding their gears, and coughing. Their seeming difficulties motivated me to leave my car at the station and walk to the court-

house two blocks away. From there I could walk
home, another six blocks, and pick my automobile
up later. Had I been on my toes, I would have called
Sara from the truck stop, to tell her to close the office and go home. Then I'd have crawled into my
car and gone home, too. It was only a few minutes
after three, but for all practical purposes, the workday was over. Doubtless, some departments in the
courthouse were already closed for the day. Each
department head has the authority to close up at his
own discretion, and a blizzard coming out of the
north is usually all the reason needed to lock the old
building up tight. But like a fool, I was on my way
to the office to keep it open until the magic hour—
four-thirty.

. There was nothing moving on Twelfth Street between Colfax and Prairie, although the street was
well lighted by lights from storefronts, and would
have provided better passage than Colfax, which
was choked with snow and stalled vehicles. Suddenly, there was something moving on Twelfth—a
black sedan hurtling at me from Prairie Avenue,
causing me to jump for the shelter of a parked car.
Cursing, I started across the street toward the
courthouse. Having pulled into an alley beside the
dime store, he backed out to come at me again, this
time leaving no doubt of his intentions. He missed
me again, and as he passed I got my pistol, jerked
the slide back to cock it, and fired three shots at the
car before it disappeared into the storm. Then, out
of the maelstrom came a clap of thunder, followed
by lesser, reverberating claps, and rushing out to
Colfax, dodging oncoming lights, I reached the
black vehicle. It had slid head-on into our new post-
office building, a small but sturdy structure of brick

and steel. The car was a Valiant, license number 25H2964, and inside the crumpled sedan a body was slumped over the steering wheel. There was a hole as large as an apple in the windshield over the wheel, obviously put there by the man's head as his car hit the brick wall. From the hole splintered cracks ran out in all directions like a bloody sunrise. The body had no pulse.

Chances are that if the man's seatbelt had been fastened, his head would not have hit the glass and he would not have died. Certainly he would not have died of gunshot wounds, because there was no indication that even one of my shots had hit the car, much less the man in it. Reaching into his jacket, I extracted his billfold to find out who he was. You are probably way ahead of me. Yes, it was Brian Keelan of 1042 Hickory Street, Winnebago City. He was five feet eleven inches tall and weighed one-eighty. The man was thirty-six years old, not very old to make the final trip. But then it had been his choice, not mine.

There was a Mannlicher bolt-action rifle lying on the back seat under an army blanket, and a twenty-two caliber Colt Woodsman pistol in the glove compartment. The Mannlicher was the kind I had always coveted but could not afford. Almost subconsciously, I turned off the ignition so that the battery of the car would not run down, then getting out of the mess, I put the keys into my pocket and pressed the little button on the door so that the car would lock when I slammed the door shut. The dead suspect was now locked in, safe from curiosity seekers until tomorrow.

Drawn by sounds of the crash, loud enough to be heard even above the howl of blizzard, curious citizens began to come out of their storm cellars and cubbyholes to see what was going on. Peering out the window of his barbershop next door to the post office, Snooks Hunter shaded his eyes with a magazine. After a time, driven by curiosity, the long-nosed barber put on his overcoat, pulled the fur collar up around his neck, and came out into the storm, calling, "What the heck happened? What's going on out here?" Because the car was so close to his door, the barber had to squeeze to get through. And nobody paid any attention to him.

When the town marshal, old Irv Glotz, finally arrived, he didn't know what to do. Like many small-town peace officers, Irv is more at home chasing drunks out of saloons or picking up rabid dogs than handling anything like a bad auto accident. When Snooks told him that he had heard shots, Irv began trying to get the door of the car open, all the while cursing people who get themselves shot in such rotten weather. "I think somebody shot a hole in the windshield," he said, and I told him that the hole was from the dead man's head, where it hit the glass when his car hit the building.

"How do you know he's dead?" the old guy demanded.

"Easy—no pulse. If you don't have a pulse, you're dead."

"Oh." Then he asked, "Did you call the fire department, Felix?"

"No. Where's the fire?"

The marshal brushed snow off his parka with one hand, while spotting his flashlight into the car with his other hand. "Damn it, I know there ain't no fire, but the volunteers have a rescue team."

"Mr. Glotz," I said patiently, "this man does not

need a rescue squad, he needs an undertaker. He's dead. Here, take his car keys. I locked him in to protect him from curiosity seekers and nosy citizens.''

"What the hell am I supposed to do with him?" the marshal asked. ''The damn undertaker is out of town, and I doubt that his goofy assistant is going to come out into a blizzard to pick up a stranger who tried to knock over our post office.''

"That," I told him, " is *your* problem, Irv—one of the awesome responsibilities of being town marshal. But, since you ask me, I'll tell you what I'd do if I were you.''

"What's that?''

"Nothing.''

"Nothing?''

"Yes, nothing. Just leave old Brian here until tomorrow. He won't bother anybody, and his car is off the street.''

"It sure is," Snooks complained. "Right in front of my door.''

Irv made a decision. "We'll leave him here until tomorrow. Anybody who would come out on a day like this to get his hair cut must be out of his mind. Why don't you just lock up and go home, Snooks, like everybody else?''

"That's right," I said. "I was on my way to close my office when I heard this crash. The courthouse will be shut down for business until tomorrow.''

"Hey! You folks get away from that car!" Irv yelled. "Don't bother the dead man!''

Curious townspeople, some from the courthouse, were pressing against the car, peering into the windows at the body, sweeping it with their flashlights. They didn't pay any attention to the marshal, who finally walked away in disgust and defeat.

The barber yelled after him, "You be sure to get Clancy over here early in the morning, Irv. I don't want my customers coming in the back door!"

Clancy Depew is the town mortician, as well as the regional agent for the *Winnebago Star*, a big Win City daily. Covering Kornfeld County and the western half of Deerhorn County, Clancy makes more money selling ads and renewals than he makes in the mortuary. But the funeral home is a nice, steady sideline—one that has no problem with a lack of consumer needs.

Thinking about Clancy and about the dead man, I plodded through deepening snow across Colfax toward my office, wishing at the same time that I had a jug in my desk, as do most department heads in the courthouse.

**6**

THE WIND HOWLED all night, blowing snow down from above, and by dawn we had nearly three feet of it covering the lowlands. It drifted, piling up house-high on brush and fences and block roads where they ran through gaps in the hills. KJRZ came on the air at 5:00 A.M. to relay news of the storm, which had by then petered out, and of school closings. What it amounted to was that virtually every school in a three-county area was closed for the day. Neu Koblenz schools would open at noon. According to the state patrol, Interstate 90 was drifted closed in a few places, while 87 between Hessberg and Neu Koblenz was solidly blocked most of the way, with nothing moving. County roads were generally closed, but open in some places to four-wheel drive vehicles.

When I went out to shovel my walk and driveway, the metallic scraping of snow shovels was already in the air; along with the whining of snow blowers and racing automobile engines was evidence of snowplows in action. Shoveling wet snow, I began to stretch muscles that hadn't been worked in seven or eight months, and I knew that those muscles would be stiff and sore before nightfall. I also knew that I was going to buy a gasoline snow blower in the very near future. When you reach a certain age, it is just begging trouble to go on shoveling snow with a hand shovel. Yet another thing that I knew was that it was going to be a long day, with cold, weary travelers drifting in from four points of the compass. It happens in Hessberg two or three times a year. And, as the welfare director, as well as a member of the County Civil Defense team, I usually see it all, from the first cold, hungry motorist to the last, boozed up young reporter from Win City or Omaha, out to write a human interest story for his newspaper.

From my house at Fourteenth and Koenig, I could see both slopes of Boneyard Creek Valley, rising above the town in polar raiment. Trees sagged under wet, heavy blankets of snow, as did power lines and telephone wires. Fortunately there was no wind to sway the laden wires back and forth, to cause them to snap, leaving bare wires spitting blue fire into the brittle-cold atmosphere.

Not a creature was stirring, not even a mouse. No cawing black crow rose from blanketed forests to cruise for food. No fluffy sparrow left his bushy home to seek grain or seed. They knew the futility of looking for food in the sea of fresh snow. Later, with cattle in feedlots tramping the snow down into hardpan and dropping warm patties onto it, the little birds would be out, picking undigested bits of corn and bran from the patties. Later they would invade the feeders in hordes to steal grain and mash from the cattle as the long troughs were filled.

The wily crow would bide his time, waiting for a turkey to die of suffocation as its beak filled with ice, or for a hungry coyote to kill a rabbit and leave part of its entrails in the snow. Later in the day, jackrabbits would be caught on snow-plowed highways by fast-charging automobiles, and mangled into food fit for a crow. But now, not a creature was stirring, save man, of course, who was stirring for sure.

Only when all the cement in front of my house was clear of snow did I return to the sanctity of the kitchen for my second cup of coffee. As it was still heating on an electric warmer, there was no wait, so I had time to finish it before the telephone buzzed, as I knew it would. It was Sam McKee, our County Civil Defense director, calling to advise me of a meeting at the courthouse. Sam is also our mayor, and if you wonder how a man with a name like that gets to be mayor of a place like Hessberg, it is quite simple—nobody else was willing to take the job. Besides, he is a Dienstbier on his mother's side, and a very nice person. We are all grateful to him for accepting the job, which does not pay anything, and takes a lot of time away from his business. To earn a living, Sam runs an International Harvester agency. He sells and services trucks and farm equipment. He does get a few dollars a month in his capacity as Civil Defense director. But that, too, takes him away from his shop, where he could make considerably more money in the same time.

My wife came up from the basement where she was washing clothes. "Where's the car—did you lose it again?"

That was an unkind dig dating back three years to a time when I had driven the car to work, then walked back and forth for several days. When Ellen needed the car on Saturday to go for groceries, it was not in the garage where it was supposed to be. It took me ten or fifteen minutes to recall that I had driven the car to work on a Wednesday and had not

seen it since. Luckily, nobody wanted the old
clunker enough to steal it, because it would not
have been missed until Saturday.

"Don't be a wise guy," I said. "I left it at the
truck stop."

"Well," she warned me, "don't forget where it is.
We may need it someday."

That gives you some idea about how acid my dear
wife can be at times. There are times, of course,
when she is very nice.

Before leaving home I called the Heffner place to
ask Frankie to look in on Old Man Miller, to see that
he had enough wood in the house to keep his fire
going all day. It was not a day when a man that age
should be wandering around outside, digging in the
snow for chunks of wood. The kid assured me that
he had already been across the street with a pot of
hot coffee and a sack of goodies, and that he had
stacked enough wood in the Miller house to last two
or three days. That pleased me, but did not surprise
me as the Heffners had kept an eye on the old guy
for years. What they didn't know was that he kept
an eye on them, too.

Because it was virtually impossible to travel on
the sidewalks, which were not shoveled clean in
front of every house, I took to the street, which had
received some wheeled traffic. If nothing else, I
could walk in tire tracks, placing one foot ahead of
the other, like a tightwire walker. Koenig was un-
plowed, but Fourteenth was open, having been
cleared by one of our two elderly snowplows. Prog-
ress was reasonably good, but now and then I had to
step off the road into waist-high snow to avoid being run down by passing vehicles. When I got to
Twelfth and Colfax, the dead man's car was still

blocking the barbershop door and a few feet of the walk. By some good fortune, the post-office door was not affected by the wreck. It was bad enough to have the barbershop blockaded. If there is anything that upsets people in a small town, it is to have the door of their post office blocked. Come hell or high water, wind or snow, the post office must be kept open. People who never mail anything but subscriptions to the Reader's Digest, and never receive anything but the Sears-Roebuck catalog, will raise all kinds of hell if their post office opens ten minutes late or closes ten minutes early.

Snooks Hunter stood at the door of his shop, fussing and fuming, cursing Irv Glotz, who probably was riding a snowplow someplace in town, not worrying about the dead stranger in front of Snooks's place. If you don't know it, small-town marshals do more than keep the peace. They pick up stray dogs, read water meters, mow weeds and plow snow, among other things.

Spotting me, the barber yelled, "How do you like his guts—leaving that corpse in front of my shop, blocking my door? Cannot even get in and out of my own place of business! If it was somebody I knew, it might be different."

"Use the back door," I suggested. "This is an emergency situation. Depew may be holed up someplace out in the boondocks, and Glotz is busy clearing snow out of the damn town."

"I *do* use the back door," Hunter whined. "But what about my customers? Man, you can't expect a person to come in the back door of a barbershop to get their hair cut." His Adam's apple bobbed comically in the scrawny neck.

"Why not?" I asked. "They used to come in the

back door when you were bootlegging." I looked
into the car, to be sure that Brian was still there. He
was, looking very peaceful, indeed. Then, looking
both ways on Colfax, I started across, crunching my
feet in the firm snow. The street was cleared for
two-way traffic, but there was no parking as snow
had been pushed up in high eskers at the edge of the
street.

Sara was in the office, as I knew she would be,
and I told her to call the secretaries and tell them
not to come in. I called Fanny myself to tell her to
take the day off because I could handle emergencies and routine business could wait for clearing
away of the snow. Louis Post, I knew, was out in
the country, no doubt holed up with some little lady
friend. With the storm as an excuse, he would stay
as long as possible. Fanny and the stenos had probably been hanging around the house, waiting for us
to call and tell them not to come in.

Using my authority as an officer of the defense
council, I told Sara to call every department head of
the courthouse and tell them to close for the day.
There wouldn't be much business transacted anyplace in the building, and it was just nonsense for a
couple of hundred people to take up what parking
space might be available on the streets. The main
idea was to keep people off the streets with their
cars, to prevent minor traffic accidents that would
tie up snow-removal vehicles. While Sara was placing the first of her official calls, I went upstairs to
the civil defense office, where some of the other officers were already gathered.

Right here, it should be explained that civil
defense alludes not only to attack from distant phil-
osophies of government, but also to attack from the

elements. In case of flood, fire, tornado or blizzard, your civil defense, like your National Guard, is organized, concerned and ready to move. You hear people sneer at the guard. They are referred to by pseudosophisticates as weekend warriors, strike-breakers, draft dodgers and other things often considered to be objectionable. But our National Guard has saved our bacon on more than one occasion. They took it on the chin in North Africa, Corregidor, Guadalcanal and Omaha Beach, for instance. Immediately prior to World War II, we had a standing army of one hundred sixty-five thousand, compared to Hitler's and Hirohito's millions. Without the National Guard and other reserve units we'd have been up the creek without a paddle. They provided the skeleton around which the meat and muscle of an army was born. God bless them!

Hal Purviance, our only county board member living in town, was in the meeting room as was Lenny O'Shay in his National Guard suit. He is a captain in the provost section.

"I suppose we should close the courthouse, except for emergency services," Purviance said, looking directly at me, and I advised him that it was being taken care of.

"The next thing," O'Shay said pompously, "is to call the radio station in Neu Koblenz and ask them to make spot announcements warning motorists to stay out of the area until further notice."

"A very good idea," I told him. "Why don't you take care of that, Captain?"

"I will," he promised. "Also, as a member of the defense council and an officer in the Guard, I have taken the liberty of asking the armory at Neu for a chopper. It will be here in an hour."

"Say," Purviance told the lawyer, "you are right on the ball, Lenny, baby!" He winked at me.

Len swelled up a little, and I suggested that maybe the radio station should be asked to advise everybody in the three-county area to check on his neighbors to see whether anybody needed help. So often, during the course of a natural disaster, there is somebody about to suffer a heart attack or a burst appendix. Or some woman is ready to deliver a baby—stuff like that.

Kurt Hohenstein came stomping in, crying, "Jesus Christ, it's cold enough to freeze the balls off a brass monkey!"

And behind him, ears red with frostbite, came the county superintendent of schools, John Brownell, who complained, "Oh, boy, it's colder than a well-digger's ass!"

The clichés dispensed with, we sat around a scarred conference table to plot a course.

"Where's old Sam, our fearless leader?" Lenny asked, smiling slightly at his own wit.

"Hey, I thought you were going to call the radio station," I reminded him.

"Oh, yeah—I knew I was supposed to be doing something."

Still grinning, he left the room just as Sam came in, saying, "Colfax is clear all the way from city limit to city limit. Irv expects to have the side streets clear by nightfall."

"There is a helicopter coming from Neu Koblenz," I told him. "This building is closed except for emergencies, and O'Shay is called KJRZ with a request for spot announcements to keep cars out of the area and to ask people to check on their neighbors."

"Sounds like a winner," he said, grinning broadly.

"And I have a suggestion."

"Yes?"

"Old Irv and the kid who helps him are not going to be able to get these streets cleared without help. All they have are a couple of rickety trucks with blades on the front. If they don't break down before the job is half done, I'll put in with you."

"What are you suggesting, Felix?"

"That you call the governor's office and get him to activate a couple of those four-by-fours parked in the Guard garage down on Sixteenth and Prairie. They have blades that can be bolted on in twenty minutes, and guardsmen to drive the rigs."

O'Shay, who had returned from making his telephone call, butted in. "Felix is right, Sam. I'll call the governor if you want me to."

"I'll do it," the mayor said hastily, looking around for a telephone. "Damn it, why don't we have a phone in here?"

"Use mine," I said. "Sara's in the office. She'll place the call for you."

"Right," he said, heading for the stairway.

We held up the meeting until Sam got back, then Brownell gave his report. "The high school is ready. Some of my teachers are standing by, and the ladies of the legion auxiliary are getting the kitchen ready. They have thirty pounds of bacon, a gross of eggs, and plenty of coffee. They need flour and shortening for hotcakes."

"Tell them to get it at Hoffschneider's and charge it to the welfare department," I said, glancing at one of my bosses, Hal Purviance, for approval. He nodded, as I knew he would. My bosses, the county board of supervisors, are easy to work with. During emergencies I can just about write my own ticket.

"There is one immediate problem," I told the assembly.

"What's that?" John wanted to know.

"Who is going to move that corpse from in front of Snooks Hunter's barbershop? His customers have to go in the back door, and Snooks does not even know the man."

"His name is Brian Keelan," Kurt said, gazing at me narrowly.

"Yes, I know. But he and Snooks have never been formally introduced. Besides that, the car is blocking the sidewalk."

"Well, we don't want strangers hanging around the barbershop," Sam McKee told us, smiling. "I'll send a tow truck over there to pull him to the mortuary. We can leave him in the car until Clancy gets back. He is not going to spoil in this kind of weather."

"Where is Depew?" Hal asked, looking around the room as if the funeral director might be there.

"Out in the sticks selling newspapers," Sam said. "His wife has no idea where he is or when he'll be home."

"Maybe he's dead," Brownell suggested. "Maybe he rolled into a ditch and froze to death."

Kurt gave the superintendent a hard look. "Are you kidding? Morticians don't die, John. They just bury people who do."

"Well, wherever he is, I hope to God he gets back pretty soon to lay that fellow out. It doesn't seem dignified for a dead man to lie around in a parked car two or three days, even if he *is* from out of town!"

Captain O'Shay stared at Brownell for a few seconds, then, seeming to decide that he wasn't joking, turned his gaze to the vaulted ceiling of the room.

Next, Sám had a message, having been in contact with civil defense wardens around the country by telephone. It was pretty much a rehash of what we already had. Eighty-Seven west of the river was clear, primarily because high winds had blown the snow away into eastern areas of the county. The rolling hills and valleys of East River had piled up snow until most of the roads were blocked, including 87 between Hessberg and Neu Koblenz. But snowplows from both counties were at work on 87, opening up long stretches of the highway to traffic. Interstate 90, which follows the river, was blocked in some places, but without the deep drifts that other roads were buried under. There were motorists stranded all along both highways, as well as on some county roads.

"The county and state have plows working north, south and east," Sam advised us. "Before very long, the roads will be open, and poor, lost souls will be coming into town from three directions, hungry and cold. They'll fill our motels and eating houses first, then run out of money, and head for the schoolhouse."

"You sound like the voice of experience," I said.

"After ten years," the mayor replied, "you get to know it all by heart."

"Well," the county attorney said, looking uneasy and impatient, "let's wind up here and get over to the athletic field. The chopper is going to land there in about fifteen minutes." Glancing at his wristwatch for verification, he got up from the hard chair, resplendent in his officer's uniform. Little

Lenny, in assuming the role of an officer in the United States Army, took on a sheen that his role of county attorney did not provide him.

Walking beside me down the broad stairwell of our courthouse, he said casually, "I hear via the grapevine that the state patrol is on the Heffner case."

"Yeah, I told Collins about it, and he was going to contact the criminal investigation division."

O'Shay seemed hurt. "We could handle it, Felix. If there has been a murder in Kornfeld County, Kurt and I will work on it."

"Sure," said Kurt, clomping down the stairs behind us.

"Of course you will," I told them, as we headed for the Thirteenth Street exit. "You guys laugh in my face when I tell you that Barney was murdered in cold blood, then when a little evidence surfaces to back me up, you get interested. You guys thought it was a joke last week, now you want in on it."

"I *told* you I was on the case," Hohenstein growled. "Who is this guy, Keelan, anyway? What was he doing around here with two firearms, and a paroled convict at that?"

"You won't believe me when I tell you," I replied, "but he is the rotten, low-down thing who killed Barney."

"What for?"

"Who knows? Maybe money."

"Then somebody hired him to do it."

"That follows," I said, with some sarcasm showing. "Somebody hired him."

"Who would do a thing like that?"

Lenny, Sam and Hal had gone ahead, walking quickly along Thirteenth Street in the still chill air, and I stopped dead in my tracks to answer the sheriff.

"Maybe it was his wife and her boyfriend," I said brutally. "To get rid of him, so they could screw around in complete freedom."

Turning red from neck to hairline, the big guy cried out: "What the hell is *that* supposed to mean? Are you accusing me of something?"

"Why, are you the boyfriend?"

"I see you've been talking to that old fart, Thad Miller," he growled. "Out there all the time with them damn glasses!"

"So? It's a free country. If he wants to snoop, there's no law against it. It's not nearly as bad to snoop as to mess around with some other man's wife."

"I'm not the only one who's been messing around with her," he replied sullenly. "She hands it out like she's some kind of charity!"

"Gentlemen don't kiss and tell," I said.

"Hell, I didn't know it was a secret," he said as we approached the high school. He was pouting. "Barney was no damn angel either, Obie. He was poontanging half the women in this county. If he had done his screwing at home, she might not have had to horse around with other guys."

"Indeed," I said, raising my brows as John Brownell came trotting up from behind, explaining that he had stopped at the rest room.

Inside the school, ladies of the legion auxiliary had coffee brewing in the cafeteria, and were frying bacon and eggs for a family of tourists. The ladies all wore blue gray dresses and purple overseas caps, with Post 103 stitched on them in gold thread.

Helen Schneider was the first to greet us. "Hello there. Do you fellows want some bacon and eggs?"

"No, thanks."

"We'll have hot cakes as soon as Emma gets back from the store," she promised.

"Just give me a cup of black coffee," I said, and Kurt and John hung around to drink some coffee with me.

The travelers, a young couple who looked like West River ranchers, watched nervously as we dawdled. Finally, the man of the family asked anxiously, "Have you gentlemen heard whether the road to Neu Koblenz is open? My wife has an appointment to see her doctor."

"What for?" Kurt asked maliciously, winking at me. The young wife was about eight months and seventeen days pregnant. Her belly stuck out like a basketball nailed to a barn door.

The rancher gave Kurt a hard look, but didn't answer.

"You may be able to get through by noon," I told the ruddy-faced man. "Plows are working from both ends. Why don't you folks try to relax and stay warm? If worst comes to worst, we have a small hospital and a pretty good country doctor here." That seemed to make them feel better, and they began eating the eggs and bacon at a table nearby. Two boys, about four and six, were buzzing around their parents, unaware that they were in the midst of a minor catastrophe. "There's a gym over there, dad. Can we go play some basketball or something?"

"No! Stay here."

"Why not, dad?" the blonde asked. "We'll stay out of trouble."

"We never get to do anything," added his dark-haired brother.

"Oh, I don't care. Ask your mother. Drink your cocoa first. Erik, come back here! I said drink your cocoa before you go to the gym!"

Following the eager brothers, I saw that there were no basketballs out and went over to a closed door at one side of the big room. Inside I found a basketball and gave it to the kids, who began dribbling and yelling and throwing the ball at a basket at one end of the gym.

Doc Hansen, the pretty good country doctor referred to earlier, sat at the coach's desk in a corner, eating bacon and eggs with whole-wheat toast. He had set up a dozen cots and piled some army blankets on them, waiting for the expected rush of cold and sleepy travelers. His black bag was on the desk, along with a cardboard box that was filled with medical supplies—bandages, pills and bottles of medicine.

"What say, Felix?" he asked. "How does it look?"

"Like a big day. There are people stranded all along both highways, and you know what that means. There will be freeloaders in here by the dozen. On top of that, the work crews will come in to eat, and charge the county for meals."

He grinned. "Do our public servants do such things? Uh, by the way, is there any late news on the killing?"

"Well, not exactly. But there is a dead man parked over by the post office. Maybe he did it."

"Any connection?" The doctor wiped at his egg yolks with a piece of bread, and I heard the popping sounds of a helicopter coming in.

"It's a long story, doc. I'll tell you all about it when I get back." Looking around for Kurt and Lenny, I walked quickly toward the rear door, hoping to reach the eggbeater first, knowing that it would not accommodate more than three passengers. Getting there first, I climbed in beside the pilot, a kid from Blue Springs, Lambert Ostdiek.

"Hi, Obie, anybody else going?"

"No doubt Captain O'Shay will be along," I replied. "He's the one who requested the beater."

"Oh, Captain O'Shay," Lambert grinned, as Lenny came out of the building, strutting. "*That* Captain O'Shay."

"That's the one."

Climbing in, Lenny said, "The sheriff isn't coming. We can take off any time you're ready, Major."

"Roger." The motor roared into life, the big blades whistled, and we rose from the field in a cloud of swirling snow.

"Where to?" Ostdiek asked as we rose above the dome of the courthouse.

"Where do you want to go, Felix," the attorney asked. "Anyplace special?"

"No, just out to look around generally, say east to the county line for starters."

Nodding, Lambert headed east along 87 toward Neu, and we spotted fifteen stalled cars between Hessberg and Prairie Junction. Judging from tracks leading to and from the vehicles, each of them had been visited by farmers. Whether by horseback, tractor or skis, each car had received an offer of help. Fortunately, along that stretch of highway there is a farmhouse at each mile post, so none of the stranded travelers was more than half a mile from help. If necessary, the motorists could have walked for help, although it would have been tough going in spots.

"Hey, look there!" Ostdiek cried, pointing toward the north horizon. "Adrian Fleming finally got a chance to try out his new snowmobile!"

We couldn't hear the whine of Fleming's machine above the roar of our own, but there he was, scooting over the great ocean of snow like a hydrofoil over Lake Erie, sending a stream of loose snow out behind. Leaving Adrian and his machine in our wake, we passed over county snowplows as they pushed great mounds of snow off the road to allow stalled cars to start their motors and head for Hessberg, or follow the blades toward Neu Koblenz. Coming in to land at Prairie Junction, which sits just inside our county line, we could see plows working on the road in Deerhorn County.

"It won't be long now," Lenny said as we set down in front of the general store, post office and gasoline station that is Prairie Junction. "Eighty Seven will be open before noon."

An American flag whipped sharply from the top of a twenty-foot pole as we stirred up the snow. Then, when we settled on our ski runners and Ostdiek cut the engine, both flag and snow quit moving.

Ed Patalski, the postmaster, owner and self-styled mayor of the Junction waited in his driveway, which had been shoveled clean in anticipation of things to come. He smiled broadly at our approach, and when Lenny asked whether everything was all right, Ed replied, "Yeah. Me and the old lady are holed in, just eating and sleeping. I wish she was over at her sister's place and I had me a go-go girl here to keep me company."

"Always in there fantasizing, aren't you, Ed?" I said. "Heck, you wouldn't know what to do with a go-go girl if you had one."

"Well, hell, I'd just have to learn." The snaggle-toothed man giggled. "How near to open is the road, fellas?"

Major Ostdiek assured the postmaster that snow-plows were at work within two miles on either side of the Junction and that they should meet at the county line by noon.

"I been on the phone most of the morning," Ed said, cocking his head to catch the deep coughing of a laboring tractor. "Nearly every doggone farm along the highway has houseguests. They just went out there and got them. One couple refused help—told Phil Basten that they was on a hunting trip and had everything they needed—blankets, hot coffee, sandwiches." He smirked. "It's a young couple." He hesitated, peering from face to face. "Do you fellas hear a tractor?"

The tractor had been popping, beyond a hill some-place, for several minutes, and was now getting closer. Before long it came nosing over a crest of the county road, pushing a wall of snow. The snow built up in front of the big machine steeply, held there by a wooden platform bolted to the vehicle at an angle. As the high-wheeled Case 400 charged forward, the snow slid off to one side of the road so that in pass-ing, the tractor left a clean path more than wide enough for a car or truck. Coming at us inexorably, the snorting red and green monster finally arrived at the gas pumps, where it sat idling while the wizened driver, swathed in a khaki parka and elbow-length fur mittens, jumped down, yelling, "Hi there, Obie; hi, O'Shay. Who's the young guy with you?"

Foxy Diller was just kidding around, because Lambert Ostdiek is his nephew.

"How's your mom?" he asked. "How come you guys are all dolled up in your soldier suits? Don't tell me we are in another damn war! Who is it this time, Iceland?"

"National Guard," Lenny crowed. "In time of emergency, you can depend upon your National Guard, Mr. Diller."

"And civil defense," I added.

"And civil defense," Lenny repeated.

Lambert laughed at us. "Don't forget the friggin' civil defense, Uncle Aaron. Are you gentlemen ready to go home?"

"Let's go," said the captain, strutting toward the chopper, with his silver bars gleaming in the sunlight. "Aaron," he mumbled, "Aaron. All my life I've been hearing about Foxy Diller. Never did I dream that his name was Aaron."

"A rose by any other name is as sweet," I told him. "Foxy fits him to a tee."

"Right," Lambert said, as he lifted the big bird off the ground. "He is foxy, indeed."

On the alert for distress signals, but seeing none, we flew back to town, which by then was coming alive like some giant anthill buried in salt overnight, with hungry insects bursting forth in the sunshine to scramble for something to eat. I was pleased to note that the black sedan had been removed from in front of the barbershop, and that a couple of National Guard trucks with blades on the front were helping Irv Glotz clear the streets.

Landing on the schoolyard, we saw a dozen out-of-town cars parked on the lot behind the gym, and when we went in, there was a great deal more ac-

tivity than there had been when we left. Some of
the teachers had come down and were entertaining
children with games. The kids, probably cooped up
in stalled cars for hours, were enjoying themselves,
running, squealing, throwing balls and bean bags.

In the kitchen, our chubby ladies of the legion
were still frying bacon and eggs as well as hotcakes,
and there was a large dixie of stew simmering on a
back burner. The cafeteria hummed with the voice
of weary travelers, exchanging horror stories of the
blizzard while eating and drinking. A few still shiv-
ered with accumulated cold.

Mayor McKee, who had been on the telephone
most of the morning coordinating snow removal,
advised us that Highway 87 was open west all the
way to the state line, and that it would be open east
to Neu in a matter of minutes. Interstate 90, across
the county, was open, and there was little or no
snow south of Mormon Crossing. The snow had
petered out near the great bend of the Deerhorn
where it turns east toward Neu Koblenz and Win
City. There were people stalled with dead motors
on the stretch between Hessberg and the rim of the
mesa, but the people were in town, and their cars
would follow shortly, as available tow trucks were
able to get to them.

After some hotcakes and coffee, Ostdiek and
O'Shay prepared to fly down the Deerhorn and
back to see what was going on there. They asked me
to go, but I had other things to do. Although the
courthouse was officially closed, there would be
emergencies in my office. So, once they were air-
borne, I finished my coffee and got started, not for
my office first, but to the mortuary to have a look at
Brian. To tell the truth, I did not so much wish to

see Mr. Keelan as to check his car for possible clues. When I got to the mortuary, Depew still had not come in from his sales trip, but Brian was in the funeral parlor, having been carried in by some obliging citizen at the behest of Clancy's wife and bookkeeper, Althea. That left the wrecked car unlocked for me, and I nosed around in it, looking for evidence.

In fiction, the police always scrape mud off a dead man's shoes or shake weeds out of his cuffs. Then the head investigator makes a speech indicating that this particular type of soil or that specific kind of weed is found only on the Smith farm, south of town, or on the Jones estate, north of town. This is stretching it a bit thin in Kornfeld County, and probably in most other counties, but you get the idea. Not that I was looking for weeds or mud—just any little thing that might be a lead. In the movies a private eye may find a matchbook cover with a telephone number in it. He calls the number, and it turns out to be the dead person's bookie or girl friend. From there, it's easy. I suppose that what I really hoped to find was a note from some enemy of Barney's, offering Keelan a contract. But there was nothing in the car. Even the rifle and the pistol had been taken out. Idly, I hoped that the Mannlicher would be put up for auction and I could get it. Inside I had no better luck with Brian than with his car. With Althea's permission, I searched his clothes, finding nothing but a dirty hanky and nine dollars in cash.

# 7

OUR LOCAL WEEKLY is the *Hessberg Hesperus*, a high-flown name for a miserable little rag of a newspaper run by a white-maned, Victorian character, Horace Mann Himberger, whom I have always suspected of being a child molester. Most weeks the big news is that Sadie Bright Eyes was home from Winnebago City for the weekend, or that Erma Eager had a letter from her son who is in the Peace Corps overseas and consequently an expert on foreign policy—things like that. So it was with some surprise that I got the story of the big fire from the *Hesperus*, even before it made the air on KJRZ. It may have been because the radio station was so busy with the blizzard and its aftermath that they did not hear about the fire. As for the *Star*, they don't print such localisms except as fillers a week or two after the fact. But the *Hesperus* played it up big, using half the front page: Grain Elevator Destroyed in Blaze! The story went on to tell how, during the fierce blizzard of Tuesday night, unseen by human eye, an elevator at the Braunholz Grain Storage Company had caught fire. The fire had destroyed a quarter million bushels of corn. Raging winds, according to Himberger, had served the double purpose of fanning the flames and keeping any possible witness inside his home. Further, blowing snow had masked the flames, in all likelihood making them invisible at a distance. It was only a miracle, the *Hesperus* stated, that adjacent elevators were not fired. The chief reason they were not, perhaps, was that the burning elevator was at the east end of the line, with winds of gale proportion blowing from the northwest. That is what the paper said. The death of Brian Keelan, normally the kind of thing to get a column on the first page, was on page 2: Win City Man Dies in Storm. Old Horace Mann must have been chagrined to have two front page stories— three, counting the blizzard—for one issue. His last previous scoop was in 1963, when the pig-knuckle cannery at Mormon Bend went out of business.

The story on Keelan said only that he was thirty-seven years old, from Winnebago City, and was killed in an auto accident when his car hit the post office. It was just another of many human interest stories arising from the storm—the couple who sat out the storm in their car near Prairie Junction; the family from an eastern state that spent the day with the Oscar Minor family two miles east of Blue Springs, and were delighted with our western hospitality; a Poland China sow on the Jody Wagner farm that chose the day of the blizzard to give birth to eighteen piglets in a hay mow—that kind of stuff.

It annoyed me in a way that I had to get the story from the paper, after spending twelve hours in town on Wednesday, and part of that time flying over it in a helicopter. I didn't see the ruins of the elevator, didn't smell the refuse, didn't hear anybody talk about it. It was even more amazing because I was in civil defense. By some farfetched series of events, I simply had not heard about it. True, I was absorbed in problems of the storm, of

the Keelan incident, and of the welfare department. But even at that, it was almost unbelievable
that in a place like Hessberg I had not been aware of
the fire until after reading about it in our weekly
newspaper.

So old Jack Braunholz burned down one of his
elevators! People always say that, even when it
isn't true. A house will burn down, destroying
everything that a family owns—clothing, furniture,
personal effects—and all their friends and neighbors will wonder how much insurance the family
had, and will begin to suspect them of arson. Sometimes the victims do not have any insurance at all,
but that does not necessarily allay suspicion.

In this case, it would seem that old Jack would
have little to gain from destruction of the building
and grain. The corn belonged to the government,
and although Jack owned the elevator, he had
nothing to gain from its burning. In an era of gallop-
ing inflation, it would cost considerably more to
replace the structure than it had cost originally, and
probably more than it was insured for. I caught myself hoping that the loss of the elevator would not
result in a concurrent loss of jobs. It takes a crew of
men to operate even one elevator, mostly in the
loading and unloading. This would be the biggest
loss immediately, unless Braunholz could use the
displaced men someplace else. A working person in
our town can less afford to lose his job than an
elevator operator of Jack's status can afford to lose
an elevator, or the federal government can afford
to lose two hundred and fifty thousand bushels of
grain. To Jack and Uncle Sam, it's a paper loss. To
the laborer, it means the loss of meat and spuds,
shoes and gasoline. It is the difference between
marginal living and sheer panic.

After reading the *Hesperus* I glanced over the morning *Star*, including the market page to get the current price of corn—two dollars and thirty-six cents a bushel on the Omaha market, indicating that about a half million dollars worth of corn had been lost in the flames. Wow!

Ellen was grumpy at breakfast, waiting impatiently for the day when her sons would be home, halfway sore that I was spending so much time out of the house on Barney's case. My wife would go through hell for a member of her own clan, but is more than a bit cool toward the problems of other people. As far as she is concerned, Barney is dead. We sent flowers and went to the funeral, and that is that. Aside from that, she had taken to referring to me sarcastically as Mr. Holmes (Sherlock), and Dick (Tracy). Dear Ellen, despite her many sterling qualities, has a childlike sense of humor. She is one of those television viewers for whom canned laughter was invented. She gets nearly hysterical over the "Lucy" show, and Red Skelton is her favorite standup comic.

"I saw a great mystery on TV last night," she told me, "an old Alfred Hitchcock rerun with Claude Rains."

"Sounds interesting," I said, waiting for the punch line.

"I haven't seen a good movie in a long time, Felix. Maybe we could drive down to Win City sometime and take in a first-run picture, or go to one of those dinner theaters. We could have a nice supper and see a show at the same time."

"Sounds like a winner," I told her. "Count me in."

She tried to pin me down. "When—this weekend?"

"How about next weekend?" There, she had me pinned.

When I left for work, sidewalks were clear and trees dripped water as a warm south breeze pushed against their blankets of snow. Crossing streets, I walked in slush that squeezed over the soles of my shoes, making me wish that I had worn my galoshes. But once in the office, my shoes would dry, and I would stay in the building all day, authorizing relief orders. Based upon past history, there would be a flood of requests for emergency relief. Many people who don't really need help tend to take advantage of the situation when natural causes bring on minor inconveniences. Aside from that, there are always people truly in need, and so often a storm will hold up the mail for a day or two, bringing real hardship to those who rely upon the post office to deliver their monthly checks—social security, private pensions, veterans' compensation or welfare. Most poor people live so close to economic disaster that a flood or a blizzard, by holding up the mail, can actually deprive them of food. For people who work at marginal jobs, living from payday to payday, an act of nature can be even more cruel. It can result in the loss of jobs, as in the construction business or farm labor. In such cases, a family, however improvident, must be taken care of. They have to eat and must have someplace to sleep and something to wear. If ill, they must have medical care. So I went to work, prepared to be inside all day. Sara and the secretaries were already there, as was Fanny Brodus. She was holed up in the office that she shared with Post, catching up on paperwork, of which there is an inordinate amount in our business. For all I knew, the redoubtable

Louis Post was still out in the boondocks—hopefully at the bottom of a canyon, buried in snow.

Linda and Linda don't touch a key on a typewriter until precisely eight o'clock. In this, as in name and age, they are identical. In all other things, they are poles apart. Smith is a scrawny brunette with acne, while Krane is a chunky blonde with the skin of a ripe nectarine. I was going to say peach, but she has no fuzz on her face. It is, like a nectarine, bare of hair and nearly bare of expression. Indeed, when Miss Krane gets going on a piece of bubble gum, she reminds me precisely of a white-faced heifer chewing her cud.

In name and age they are the same for the simple reason that almost every baby girl born in our county that year was named Linda. Three-fourths of all the girls in their graduating classes were Lindas. Three-fourths of those graduating the year before were Kimberly. So now you know what year the blizzard hit Hessberg—twenty years after Kimberly. Anyway, the Lindas do not stay long. The Linda Smiths usually run off to distant cities to go to work for big insurance companies and grow old on company bowling teams. The Linda Kranes get pregnant before they really learn the office routine, and they get married and move to rural Blue Springs or Hanover to begin the manufacture of little farmers in wholesale lots. Our office, like most other public offices in small towns, functions as a way station for local girls leaving high school and going on to their appointed destinies. A few, like Sara, linger on to provide the backbone of our community. Without our Saras, the rural government could not possibly survive.

Then, we have our second line of defense, the

Fannys—no pun intended. These are the married professional women whose husbands can't keep them busy at home or can't support them adequately. These women don't like the make-believe, busy-busy volunteer organizations designed by rich men's wives to keep themselves out of mischief.

Our Fanny is something else again—one of the *doggy* people. She loves them and raises them. There are twenty-three yapping, bouncing cocker spaniels in a chicken-wire enclosure behind the Brodus house. Some of them are champions or near-champions, as judged at various dog shows around the country. Fanny spends her weekends and summer vacations showing dogs, going as far as Denver or Rapid City and back in three or four days, just to participate in a show. Her home, just outside town near the river, is a study in dog-dom. Walls of the living room are lined with pictures of dogs and dog handlers. Some of the photos have red, blue or white ribbons stuck to them, honoring the dogs, and there are dogs embroidered on the towels in their john. Truthfully, I have always felt a little sorry for Benny Brodus, who loves his wife, but hates dogs. He must be one of the most frustrated, miserable men in the county.

Not content with filling her home life with dogs, Fanny has them in her office—pictures, that is, sitting on her desk as pictures of children sit on the desks of other people.

Aside from all this, Fanny is a very good case-worker, with compassion for people less fortunate than herself, but with sense enough to prevent her being a starry-eyed do-gooder. She gets a full one hundred pennies out of the taxpayer's dollar. So while I don't share her enthusiasm for her cocker spaniels, I do treasure her as a member of my little staff.

"Good morning," I greeted her, "I see that you got out of the blizzard in one piece. How did your dogs survive the weather?" Not that I really cared how her dogs survived the weather. It is just that it is easier to get down to business with Fanny once she has warmed up. And there is no quicker way to warm her up than to show some interest in her dogs. Doggy people are like that. So are horsey people, but you have to talk about horses.

Brodus, who is a stocky, fiftyish woman with jet-dyed hair, responded quickly, "Jeepers, no problem at all, Obie. Their shed is tight and solid. The thermostat keeps it at a steady sixty-five—but they just loved the blizzard. It seemed to bring out all the atavistic instincts of their heritage."

"It did?" I asked. "That sounds exciting—atavistic instincts—wow!"

"Did you hear the explosion?" she asked. "Our dogs heard it, and nearly went wild."

"What explosion?"

She busied herself, stacking up files of clients whom she meant to see that day. Satisfied that they were in proper sequence, she answered me. "The elevator—the big silo that blew up the other night."

"Oh, I didn't know it blew up...I thought it *burned* up."

Staring at me goggle-eyed, she said: "It did both, boss. First it blew, then it burned."

"Very interesting. Did you and Benny go to the fire?"

"Are you kidding—in that storm? In fact, we didn't know at the time what it was. We thought that a train might have derailed or a plane might have crashed in the storm."

"Didn't you see the fire?"

"You couldn't see a fire at that distance, with the snow whipping like that. Jeepers, I could hardly see to feed the dogs Tuesday evening." Having selected and sorted her files, she put them into a square, no-monkey-business attaché case and got up to leave. Slipping into a blanket-lined parka, she expressed some hope that she could get through to Wells, then walked with me into the reception room, where Sara had two emergency cases waiting for me. The first was a family group consisting of a couple in their early thirties and three boys, who seemed to be about six, eight and ten years old. The boys wore low shoes, bib overalls and worn, cut-down army coats. Their father was similarly dressed while their mother was in wrinkled, men's woolen pants under a pleated skirt, and soiled, white tennis shoes. To complete her wardrobe, she had on a plaid shirt and heavy white letter sweater with a big, red "C" on the front. The entire family was thin, and blond to the point of being albino.

Motioning them into my office, I closed the door and asked them to sit down. Then, addressing myself to the man, I asked, "What is your name, sir?"

"Calvin Jorgensen."

"Where are you from, Mr. Jorgensen?"

"Cedartown." He answered my questions warily, as if I were out to get him.

"That's in Cedar County," I said, wondering why he had not gone to his own county for help. "What kind of work do you do?"

"Farming," he mumbled, "but I can't get no work anyplace."

"He just got out of the pen," his wife told me, showing more spirit. "Nobody will hire him in Cedar County. The kids and I were on A.F.D.C., but the minute Cal got home, they cut us off."

"When was that?"

"October 29. The day after he got home." She began to cry softly.

"What did you get sent up on?" I asked Jorgensen, who was bent over, staring at the floor.

"A bad check. I gave it to a guy and asked him to hold it until the first of the month."

"A bar owner?"

"Yeah, Manny Norgard, over home. He held checks for me before."

"Why didn't he hold that one?"

"Well, he got sick and wound up in the hospital in Neu, and his old lady ran the check through. It was just one of them things."

"Mrs. Norgard is not a nice person," Mrs. Jorgensen explained. "Manny is all right, but his wife is sort of a—"

"A bitch," her husband finished.

"I assume it wasn't the first one that bounced on you," I said, looking at him closely.

Returning my gaze, he told me, "No, it wasn't, but you can bet your butt it will be the last one." He sounded convincing. "I did eight months in the penitentiary on a measly ten-dollar check, and my wife and kids was living on welfare like animals!" He was angry.

So was I. This is one of the inconsistencies in our society. A bar owner, eager to sell a drink, will cash a check for any Tom, Dick or Harry who walks in. Then when the check bounces, he calls for a cop. In many cases the man goes to prison after a costly court trial, and his family goes on welfare. To satisfy the ire of a woman bilked out of ten dollars, the Jorgensen family had cost the taxpayers thousands of dollars over a period of some nine months, and had in the bargain just about lost their credibility. It is my feeling that anybody who cashes a bad check should either eat it or share the guilt. It takes two to tango. That is not to absolve the felon of blame—only to place things in perspective.

I asked Calvin what he could do on a farm, and he boasted that he could do it all—chores, haying, milking, feeding, tractor driving, trucking, you name it.

"Would you work for five hundred a month, plus a house, fuel, milk, eggs and meat?"

"Would you accept an all-expense-paid tour of the South Pacific?" he countered, grinning wryly.

"I had one in 1942 and 1943."

He looked interested. "You did?"

"But they had another name for it. They called it World War II."

"Oh." He seemed disappointed.

Reaching for my telephone, dialing Fred Cherek, I studied the miserable little family, sitting so stiffly on the hard, wooden chairs of my office, the boys too weary and chilled to scuffle in sibling rivalry as they might normally be expected to do.

"Hello," said a voice on the wire, "Fritz Cherek here."

"This is Felix, Freddy. Is that job still open?"

"What job is that?"

"Didn't you want a married man on your feed-lot?"

"Oh, yeah! My son-in-law has been helping me out, but we're both fagged. This damn storm has been harder on us than on the cows. Why, have you got somebody?''

"Could be. This fellow is from Cedar County, a wife and three kids. Lots of farm experience.''

"Sounds good, Felix. What's the gimmick?'' He sounded dubious.

"No gimmick at all, but this man just got out of the pen on a check charge—did eight months. If you hire him, it will have to be on that basis. I don't want you to have any reservations.''

"Oh, hell, Felix, come on. Give me a little credit, will you? What does a phony check have to do with feeding cows?''

"Nothing. But some people would make a connection.''

"Listen, I can use the man right now. How soon can you bring him out? I got work piled up until hell won't have it.''

"We'll be there within an hour," I promised. "Is the road open?''

"Yeah, yeah. Meet me at the little house where Joe Kaminsky used to live—you know, *old* Joe. See you in an hour, Felix.''

"Well, you have a job," I told Cal Jorgensen, feeling pleased with myself. "Now, let's get you some groceries and something to wear. You boys open up that closet and see what you can find.''

The closet is always full of used clothing, collected throughout the year from church rummage sales and spring housecleanings. Much of it is old-fashioned and out of style, but clean and serviceable. It beats going naked. Pulling out boxes of shoes and boots, the kids began to fit themselves with warm footwear. When they were shod, they went through the closet in search of shirts, pants, jackets and gloves.

While they were dressing themselves, I was calling the welfare office in Cedartown to talk with the director, Franz Hober, a stiff-backed veteran of the Dinosaur School of Social Work, who immediately saw something funny about my call. That is typical of the Dinosaur school, which assumes that any needy person is a lazy person, that every poor person is a borderline criminal, that help in time of need is charity. Hober is a classic example of the narrow, insensitive welfare director who bounces disadvantaged people from county to county, from agency to agency, keeping them ever at the mercy of self-righteous, arrogant public servants. He chortled into my earphone. "My, my, so you have the Jorgensen family in Hessberg, Felix. Well, I guess our loss is your gain. We hate to lose a prominent family like the Jorgensens, Mr. Oberstdorf." He laughed nastily.

"Then you will be delighted," I told him, "to learn that you have not lost them."

"What do you mean?" He sounded fearful, suspicious.

"What I mean, Mr. Hober, is that I am filling their tank with gasoline and sending them back to you right now." I winked at Calvin, whose face was showing alarm.

"Why would you want to do that?" Hober asked, and I could almost see his strained, dark face in my telephone. "Just fill their tank, buy them some cheese and crackers, and send them on to Butte County. They can work their way to the coast like that." He chuckled. "I call it the overground railway."

"But," I reminded him, "if they go back to Cedar County, they can get on A.F.D.C. They can't do that on the coast until they have established residence."

"They can't get on welfare in my county," he snarled. "I just got rid of them after eight months. That damn jailbird can get a job and go to work!"

"Who is going to hire him? Do you have a job offer for Mr. Jorgensen, Franz? You cut them off welfare too fast. According to the rules, you should have kept them until January. I have taken the liberty of advising Mr. Jorgensen of his rights, and have offered him the use of my telephone to call the state office."

"His appeal would take five or six weeks," Hober scoffed.

"Indeed it would, but in the meantime, you'd be obligated to provide the family with general relief, pending a decision, which you know darn well will be in their favor. Then you will have to give them their A.F.D.C. retroactively, from this day." I had him nailed to the wall, and he knew it.

"All right, Oberstdorf, what do you want?"

What I wanted was an authorization from Cedar County to provide the Jorgensen family a hundred dollars in general relief for emergency clothing and a like amount for groceries.

Old Hober squirmed like a worm on a fish hook. He blustered and snorted in indignation, threatened me and called me names. But I held firm, until finally he agreed, saying, "I think you're a doggoned agitator and troublemaker, Oberstdorf—a discredit to your profession!"

I laughed at him and said, "Please write that down and mail it to me. Coming from you, it is a testimonial to my worth."

Without answering he slammed down his receiver. I went out to Sara's desk to have her write the relief orders, and while she was doing that, I talked to the second couple, Indians from Cedar Ridge, who were out of gasoline and money, having spent it all while delayed by the storm.

"Look," I told them, "all I can do is authorize the truck stop to feed you and gas you up so you can get home. This lady will give you an order on the Westside Café for ten dollars. That should handle it. They have a nice plate lunch for two dollars, with coffee and pie. That will leave enough for gasoline to get you home. Five gallons should be plenty unless you're driving a truck."

The young man, who reminded me a lot of my son, Earl, with his dark, intense face and angular body, laughed. "We have a truck, but five gallons will get us home, sir. It's only thirty-five miles. I'll send you the money when I get home."

"You don't have to," I said.

"We want to," the girl, who looked a lot like an Italian movie star, told me. "We have money at home."

I shrugged. "Whatever you say. Have a nice trip, and stop in and see us the next time you're in town."

The girl glanced at me quickly, thinking that I was joking, but I wasn't. They took the order from Sara and left the office after thanking us both. As I was staring after the girl, Sara gave me a funny look, and I grinned, saying, "That is the kind of girl I want my sons to bring home—the daughter I never had."

Before leaving the office I signed a handful of relief orders and told Sara to use her own judgment for the next hour, then gathered up the Jorgensens and headed for Cherek's feedlot. Both the elder Jorgensens had taken shoes and clothing from my closet, and looked warmer in heavy shoes and sheepskin jackets. I drove, and they followed me in a rattling, three-quarter ton G.M.C. that had a tarp over the bed. Kenny and Karl rode in the back under a pile of quilts, while the youngest, Kerry, rode in the cab with his parents. We stopped at Hoffschneider's long enough to pick up a few groceries, then drove out the county road, past the mental hospital, toward Cherek's place, a section of rolling farmland three miles out of town. Cherek, a grain farmer by preference, feeds out a few hundred head of steers every winter, using his own grain, with supplements. It is a small operation compared to some in the county, but he is not a poor man by any means. His overhead is low because he feeds on his own farm, using his own hay and grain, and does not put out much for labor. At five hundred a month plus extras, his hired man costs him less than seven thousand dollars a year, and all he needs is one man because he does a lot of the work himself.

The road was clear of snow, which had been pushed up to each side, forming walls six feet high that partially blocked my view of the fields. From the top of each rise, however, I could see out over the rolling, wave-capped country that looked very much like an ocean that has been quick-frozen during a typhoon.

Cherek, a giant of a man with a noble, bony nose, waited for us at the feedlot, and immediately took Cal on tour to orient him to the operation, leaving me to carry the groceries in for Mrs. Jorgensen. She was crying again, walking around the combination living room-kitchen of the little house, rattling stove lids, peering into cupboards. They had everything they needed to start a new life—stove, refrigerator, table and chairs. There was a double bed in each bedroom, and a living-room sofa that could be pulled out to make a bed. The house was like a cabin in one of our state parks, with a utility room containing a hot-water heater, shower, wash basin and toilet. Between the wash basin and shower, there was a somewhat elderly automatic washing machine.

The boys, having each consumed a candy bar and a bottle of pop during their ride out from town, and being encased in warm clothing, were in high spirits. They scampered about the place, bouncing on beds and the sofa, yelling at each other, while I was lighting a fire in the pot-belly stove that was their only source of heat. The cook stove was electric, fine for cooking, but not for heating. That is one advantage of gas. If you have to, you can help heat your house with the oven.

"Hey," I barked, "why don't you dudes stop horsing around, and go get some wood for the stove. I think I saw a pile out by the chicken shed."

Obediently the boys ran outside and began bringing in chunks of wood from the pile, and before long, they had enough to last all day. Their mother, whose name, as I eventually learned, was Nila, had put a skillet on the stove and was frying bacon. While it was frying, she took a stick of butter out of its package, and began slicing bread from a heavy, round loaf. She seemed like a different person from the one whom I had seen in my office—no longer a welfare applicant, but the mistress, the wife and mother of her own home. Having cried herself dry, she looked somehow refreshed and happy.

The boys were unloading the truck, bringing in blankets, dishes, and assorted household items, tossing them into piles along one wall of the cabin. Nila began to fry eggs, at the same time urging, "Wash up, boys, and get ready for breakfast."

"I want three eggs, mom, I'm starving," Kerry told her.

"Me, too," Kenny cried, rushing into the utility room to wash his hands and face.

"Not me," Karl told his mother, "I want four. I'm the oldest and I need more. I do the most work."

"You'll get two each," Nila said firmly. "I only bought a dozen. We have to go to the store tomorrow and get what we need."

"Don't forget," I said, "that you have a flock of laying hens here. Mr. Cherek keeps them for the hired man. I'll bet you have a few eggs in the henhouse right now."

Hearing this, Kerry slipped out, to return shortly with a stocking cap half-filled with eggs. "I got eight, mom! Now can we have three apiece?"

"Oh, I guess so. Would you like a cup of coffee, Mr. Oberstdorf? I suppose you had breakfast."

"Bright and early, Mrs. Jorgensen. Feed the boys—they've been working hard." The kids beamed at that, and their mother said, "I don't know how to thank you, Mr. Oberstdorf. We were about at the end of our rope." Her cheeks were pink from the heat of the stove, and she had some luster in her blue eyes.

"Well, the hour before dawn is the darkest," I told her, cringing at the cliché. "I'm glad to be of service. It's what I get paid for."

"I'm going to like it here. That Mr. Cherek seems to be a nice man."

"He sure is."

"Where do we go to school, Mr. Oberstdorf?" Karl asked, wolfing down his fourth egg and third slice of bread.

"The school is about a mile from here, the next corner north. It's three rooms and three teachers—all the way from kindergarten to eighth grade."

"I'm in first grade," Kerry said. "Give me some more bacon, mom."

"You've already had four," she told the boy. "We have to save some for your father."

Feeling better than I had in a long time, I went outside into the bright, warm air of the day. White Minorca laying hens clucked around in the feedlot, beneath grain bins that leaked dribbles of corn. Hens scratched at the packed snow, pecking at it to get bits of grain that had been trampled into the snow by feeding steers. Shorthorn cattle, munching hay and grain from bins, cocked their heads to gaze with mild annoyance at the hens, and far-off, in some sheltered draw, a cock pheasant raised his shrill voice in challenge.

The feeding cattle made me think of Emhoff. That in turn brought Braunholz and his elevators to mind, and it suddenly struck me as strange that the first person in town to know about the fire was the newspaper editor, a man not famed for his alertness. Also, come to think about it, wasn't it some coincidence that the silo exploded and burned during the worst blizzard in recent history—at the exact time when all evidence would be blown away and buried in snow?

With the sun beating down upon my head and the

low rumble of conversation coming to my ears from the barn, I went toward my car, leaving the Jorgensen family to begin their new life. Even in a small community like ours, when one life ends, another begins. An old man dies, a baby is born. The Heffner family dies a little, the Jorgensen family finds new life. It has to be that way, or else we could not survive.

## 8

THE DEERHORN RIVER runs across Kornfeld County from north to south, then swings east between Kornfeld and Washington Counties into Deerhorn County, past Neu Koblenz, then southeast a hundred miles to Winnebago City, our capital and largest community, with a population nearing three hundred thousand.

Near the central business district of Win City, in a bend of the river, is a square mile of small homes and narrow streets, known locally as Sicilian Flats. As the area is flat, and was settled on in the year 1905 by large numbers of Sicilian immigrants, the name was not only appropriate, but virtually inevitable. Prior to World War II, English was a second language along Third Avenue, the main drag of the Flats. Italian was the language most frequently heard in the bars, shops and churches, and Sicilian Flats had its own favorite son in the state legislature, as well as a fair share of ward heelers in City Hall. After the war, old Sicilians began to die or move to California, or even back to Sicily to retire on social security. As young Sicilians became more affluent and moved to the western suburbs, the Flats began to attract other kinds of Americans looking for cheap rent. Eventually, Sicilian Flats became an international area, inhabited by the economically deprived of all races. You rarely hear Italian spoken there anymore, the Santa Lucia festival is fading, and pizza has gone uptown.

In 1915, Pietro Petillo arrived in Win City from Palermo with his bride of six months. He was twenty years old. Lucretia was seventeen. They rented an apartment above a grocery store at Sixth and Columbia, and Pete got a job cleaning coaches for the Blue Hills and Prairie Railroad Company. In 1918 Pietro Petillo enlisted in the United States army and went to France. He came home six months later, unscratched, and promptly joined the American Legion, making it his second religion. When he died in 1962, an honor guard from Melting Pot Post 453 spread a large American flag over his coffin in East Lawn Cemetery, and fired six volleys of blank cartridges over Pete's body. Then they folded the flag according to protocol and gave it to Lucretia. She stayed on in a brick house that they had bought in 1924 for three thousand dollars. She is still there, a wizened little old woman who likes to cook for all her children and grandchildren on weekends and holidays.

Their eldest son, Angelo, was born while his father was in France. Peter and Sebastiano came along two years and four years later. They all put on the suit for the big war, and after that, Pete and Subby went to work for the railroad while Angie opted for the police department. I guess four years in uniform got him in the mood. He has been on the police force ever since. He started out riding a bike around the Flats, graduated to a one-man cruiser, then to the vice squad. He moved up from patrolman, through the ranks to captain, and if he'd had a little more political clout, he'd be the chief of police by now. But he is nearing retirement and will draw a nice pension, which is more than I can say for myself. Our retirement program is a joke.

I've known Captain Petillo a long time, since the days in Camp Robinson, Arkansas, when he had a mop of red hair and was known as Red. With the passage of time, his hair has thinned and turned gray, but he is still Red to me.

When I walked into his office Thursday afternoon, he greeted me effusively, the way many Italians do, warmly, sincerely, heartily. "Hey, Obie, what the heck are you doing in town? Sit down, boy. How's the wife and kids?" Grabbing my hand, he pumped it up and down.

The difference between a man like Red Petillo and one like Kurt Hohenstein is in the warmth. Kurt can backslap and bootlick all day long, and he is still a cold, reserved Plattdeutscher.

"Everything is fine and dandy, Red. How is it with you?"

He offered me a cigar, and I took it and put it into an inside pocket to avoid offending him. His uncle makes the cigars in his basement, and they are very good—if you like cigars.

"Fine, fine," he crowed. "My baby, Angela, is getting married in May, and you're coming down for the wedding if I have to send a cop up to get you."

I laughed at his forceful invitation. "You can always put out an A.P.B."

"What's that?"

"Heck, Red, I don't know. I see it on television all the time. A crook gets away from the jail, and the sheriff gets on his radio and puts out an A.P.B. on the guy."

"Oh, *that*. You'll have to pardon me, Obie. I've been working nights for so long that I missed all the cop shows. Now that I'm on days, I like to go to bed early."

"You're not missing anything," I assured him. "Just when you begin to think that TV couldn't possibly be any worse, it gets worse. The only thing I watch anymore is football."

That got him started on Big Blue, our state university football team, and we spent ten or fifteen minutes on that, then he invited me out to the house for supper, and I declined on the grounds that there was a storm warning out for our area and I wanted to get home before dark. That was not exactly the truth. You don't drive a hundred and twenty miles to a city famed for its restaurants, and then volunteer to eat a home-cooked meal. You can get a home-cooked meal at home. Besides, I know how a woman loves to have her husband haul in a supper guest on short notice.

"Well, what can I do for you?" he asked. "You didn't drive all the way down here in the middle of winter just to say hello."

"No, I didn't. I came down to pick your brain. Man, you're losing weight!"

"So glad you noticed," he smirked, patting his flat stomach. "Would you guess that I weighed a hundred and eighty pounds a year ago?"

"So did I."

He leaned back in his swivel chair, with his arms locked behind his head. "You did?"

"Yep—and now I weigh two hundred."

My old friend laughed dutifully at my little joke, as old friends are wont to do, then asked, "What's on your mind, buddy?"

So I told him all about Brian Keelan, and asked him for help in getting some background on the dead man.

Red frowned. "A bad gee, Felix. A punk . . . dangerous like a garbage-eating sewer rat. No guts, but a dope addict. He'd shoot you in the back for a fix, or for money to buy a fix. He's served time on burglary, armed robbery, possession of heroin. You know the type—in trouble all his life. Finally went in for murder. Keelan started out early in a broken home. His old man was an alcoholic pool hustler, his mother a kind of semipro whore. When Brian was three or four years old, his father duffied out and was never seen around here again. Chances are that he got full of canned heat and fell under a freight train. Not long after he disappeared, his wife dumped the kid on relatives, and went to Ohio with a light-bulb salesman. When he was five, he made his first institution—the county detention home. Next it was the boys' training school, then the reformatory. Finally he made the big time—the state pen."

I marveled at his knowledge of the man, just one of hundreds that Red had worked with in his years on the force. Did he have that same knowledge of every lawbreaker in the city? Hey, I remembered him from the old days—when he had trouble remembering his serial number. I asked him.

He grinned. "Of course, Obie, I have total recall—developed it in long years on the force."

"You're kidding!"

"Of course I am. The truth is, I just reviewed the case after a request for information from the highway patrol. They are doing a criminal investigation on him. It seems that he is a suspect in another possible murder case someplace."

"That *someplace* is Hessberg," I told him, "and we have old Brian up there on a slab, waiting for a county burial, unless we can dig up a friend or relative willing to provide a funeral."

Petillo laughed. "I doubt that. His friends and relatives are not the type of people to spend money that way, as you may have guessed."

"Yes, I would guess that."

"Then, why did you *really* come to Win City?" he demanded, the policeman rather than the old friend.

At that point, it seemed best to tell him the entire story, leaving out nothing. When he had it all, he got an unmarked car from the police garage and drove down Cotter to Tenth Street and south to Hickory, to the fleabag where Keelan had been living—the Avalon Hotel, room 33.

"He's been living with a broad," Red advised me as we walked along the ground floor corridor. The hall was carpeted with a very old, flowered runner that was frayed at the edges and was worn clear through in spots to show the ugly, wide-board floor beneath. The wallpaper matched, being faded and cracked, and falling away from the wall in places.

"Who is the woman?"

"Some floozy that he met in a bar—calls herself Mrs. Keelan, but she isn't."

"Man," I said, "you seem to know what's going on!"

"Just doing my thing," he answered, grinning modestly. "It's part of my job to know all the hustlers, vags and ex-cons in town. I know who they are, where they are, what they eat, and where they sleep—and with whom." Stopping at a closed door that needed paint, he grunted, "Here it is."

And he rapped sharply at the door with knuckles made tough by years of such rapping.

There was a sound of shuffling in the room, but the door did not open. Red rapped again, more insistently, and after a few seconds, the door swung inward to let us view a young woman with a forty-inch chest and a thirty-six brassiere. Her breasts pressed against each other in their confinement, striving to get out, and her pink slacks stretched gallantly on rounded hips, doing their best to not split their seams. She had a pouty mouth with a slightly protruding upper lip and wore a platinum wig. There was a tiny opal earring on each lobeless ear, and hostility in her wide green eyes.

"Mrs. Keelan?" Red asked.

She glared at us suspiciously. "Yeah—what can I do for you?"

"I am Captain Petillo of the Winnebago City police department."

"As if I didn't know," she sneered. "I can smell fuzz a mile away."

"I know," he said gently. "And this is Mr. Oberstdorf, from the Kornfeld County welfare department. We'd like to ask you a few questions, if we may."

"Like what?"

"Like, did your husband have any life insurance?" I replied, stepping past her into the room.

"That's none of your beeswax," she snapped. "That's for me to know and you to find out! You welfare guys are worse than cops!"

"That bad?" I asked.

"Thanks," Red said, all the while looking around the apartment, turning his grizzled head first one way, then the other.

"Have you got a search warrant?" the angry woman demanded.

Petillo ignored her, and I said, "Look, Mrs. Keelan, the man is on a slab in a mortuary in Hessberg, waiting to be buried. If somebody doesn't come up with funeral expenses, he's going to be put into a wooden box and a grave at the edge of our cemetery. He won't even have a marker."

"He didn't have no insurance," she said bitterly. "Who's going to sell insurance to an ex-con?"

"Plenty of people," Red told her. "Now just don't be so hostile, Mrs. Keelan—"

"Oh, cut out that crap!" she cried, glaring at him in dislike. "You know damn well we wasn't married."

"Okay," he said, "now we can get down to business. Who was his contact in Hessberg?"

"Where?" She seemed puzzled.

"In Hessberg. Who gave him the contract on Barney Heffner?"

"Man, you're crazy," she told him. "I don't know anything about any Barney Heffner or a contract. I lived with him, I wasn't in business with him."

I could see that Red was getting steamed up, and when he does that, somebody is in trouble. When we were in the service, I saw him whip loudmouths twice his own size, with adequate provocation.

"Listen, you goofy hooker," he snarled, "if you want to go on doing business in this town, you'd better stop this stupid double-talk and give us some answers!"

She pouted and sulked. "You can't make me."

"No, I can't," he agreed, "but I can make you wish to Christ you had."

"I don't know nothing about Brian's business,"

she said defensively, coming down off her high
horse. "He never told me nothing. Brian didn't
trust women."

No wonder, I told myself, thinking about Brian's
mother.

"Do you want to give me a list of his friends?"
Petillo asked kindly, shifting from his tough-cop im-
age to that of a parish priest. "Perhaps we should
notify them of Brian's passing."

She complied, reeling off names as he wrote into a
small pad that he had been holding ready, along
with a ball-point pen.

"If any of his friends want to chip in on a funeral
for Brian," I told her, handing over one of my
cards, "have them contact me."

"Okay," she said, putting the card down into her
brassiere, between tossing mounds of white flesh.
She knew that we were glancing at her chest from
time to time. Being looked at was a part of her business, and she seemed to enjoy it.

We started for the door, where Red stopped to ask
one more question. "By the way—what *is* your
name, lady?"

"Elvira Whinny," she said, "believe it or not,
Miss Elvira Whinny."

"Well, Miss Whinny," he said, "thank you very
much for your help."

"Don't mention it," she replied, getting spunky
again, "it is my patriotic duty to tell the fuzz all I
know."

"You can bet one thing," my friend told me as we
walked out of the hotel.

"Yes, what is that, sir?"

"I'll have her fat ass in jail before the week is out!
She better not jaywalk or spit on the goddamned

street. Let's stop in the bar and see what the dummy bartender has to say."

Long ago, when Winnebago City was young, the Avalon House was a luxury hotel with a covered carriageway, a six-story lobby with a spiral staircase, and an open elevator that ran up to the top floor from the lobby via twin rails. When I was a kid the elevator was still a tourist attraction. People used to stand in the lobby of the hotel, gawking at the wire cage as it rose from the ground floor, hauled on steel ropes to the ceiling, stopping at each level whether anybody got off or not. But it has been a long time since the old lift last operated at the Avalon. Around 1935, the city declared it to be unsafe and it was removed. At the same time, a false ceiling was built at the second level over the lobby, and the basement saloon, closed by Prohibition in 1919, was re-opened with Repeal.

The room, with its ornate, cut-glass chandeliers and hand-carved back bar, is still a classic for the classicists, although the Philistines who own it have let it deteriorate to a dank cave beneath the city. But for some of us, the romantic element, it is still an experience to sit in the gloomy atmosphere of the Avalon Bar and dream of another era.

My friend Angelo, however, is not a romantic. Going into the Avalon is just part of his job, giving him no cause, no pause for other considerations. Thus, he strode right up to the bar to greet the stocky, moon-faced bartender. "Hi, Steve. I want you to meet Mr. Oberstdorf from Hessberg. He's the welfare director up there."

"Glad to know you," the man mumbled, not bothering to halt his bar mopping long enough to shake hands with me. He seemed to be nervous and sullen.

"He'd like to ask you some questions," Red said, "about Brian Keelan, Mr. Kavich."

"I think he's dead," Kavich said, pinning us with his black, gimlet eyes.

"We *know* he's dead," Red replied. "We just thought that you might be able to give a lead on some of his friends."

"Nah, he just comes in—came in—and sat alone in a booth most of the time. Sometimes he had Ellie with him."

Red's ears pricked up. "Ellie?"

"Yeah—Elvira, that lady he was living with."

"Oh. Just her—nobody else?"

Before Steve could answer, a hail from a thirsty customer took him down the bar. He tossed some ice cubes into a glass, poured a shot of whiskey and a splash of seltzer over them, and picked up the money. After ringing up the sale, he returned to us, lifted a glass of beer from beneath the bar, and took a big gulp of it. Staring thoughtfully at the crud-caked, dusty chandeliers, Steve Kavich shook his head slowly from side to side, until, motivated by a hostile stare from the policeman, he admitted, "Well, he knew a few of the guys who came in—like to buy a round now and then, or shoot a game of snooker, but no real friends that I know of. He came and went alone, or with Ellie."

"This Ellie," Red said, "is she a hustler?"

"Hustler?" The man furrowed his high forehead.

"Yeah, hustler," Red told him, smiling thinly. "Hooker, prostitute—whatever terminology you care to use."

"Not here," Kavich answered, letting his indignation show. "We don't allow that stuff here."

Red studied the man coldly for a while, then told

him, "I hope not, Stephan, old thing, because we are going to be watching you from now on—real close. I ask you a few simple questions, and you play dumb. If you are not with us, then you must be against us. From now on out, watch your step. Any broad you let hang around here to solicit may be a policewoman, and any drunk you sell a drink to may be an undercover agent from my office." Red pretended to be angry and upset, but he winked at me, enjoying his tough-guy act.

The bartender scowled darkly, but didn't reply. A pair of idlers in baggy suits came down the stairs from street level, hung their coats up on wall hooks, and turned on a three-hundred-watt bulb that hung above the pool table. While one of them racked the balls, his buddy came over to the bar for two bottles of beer, and my friend Angelo said, "You know, Felix, I've been thinking about something."

"I gathered that. What is it?"

"It's too bad the fellow who owns the elevator didn't know that the fire was coming. He could have sold the corn and put the money into his pocket."

"How could he? It wasn't his corn. It belonged to the federal government."

"But," he insisted, "if somebody *had* sold the grain, nobody would be the wiser, right? That blizzard blew burning corn all over three or four counties. Who knows how much was really in the silo, except the elevator owner? It could have been two hundred thousand bushels—or two thousand, Felix. Are you going back downtown with me?"

"No," I answered, pondering his speech. "I can walk. It's only eight or ten blocks, and I want to hang around here for a while." Trophies of the hunt, spaced around the walls of the big saloon, had given me the germ of an idea. Sitting belly up to the bar, watching Red go up the steps toward Tenth Street, I asked for a gin and sour, and when Steve brought it, said casually, "Who is the great white hunter? That is a very nice eight-point head up there."

Glancing at a mounted deer head, hanging behind the bar, he admitted modestly that it was his and he had shot it in the Big Horn Mountains.

I scoffed. "All the way to Wyoming for an eight-point buck? Man, you must be kidding. My God, I've seen eight-pointers in my own backyard!"

He took the bait. It showed in his face as he rang up my drink and brought the change from a five. Glancing past him, into the mirror of the back bar, I noted that the two idlers were hard at it, cracking pool balls and razzing each other, and out on the street, I heard a bus rumble past, hissing its air brakes and revving its big engine.

"Are you trying to pull my leg?" the bartender demanded.

"What for? Why would I want to lie about a thing like that? Heck, I'm not a big-game guide, not selling anything, just a country boy in town for the day. Mr. Kavich, I live a block from Boneyard Creek, the home of so many ten-point bucks that you wouldn't believe it. We have three-hundred pounders wandering up and down the creek every day. If it were not for a town ordinance making it illegal to discharge a firearm inside the city limits, I could sit on my back porch and shoot a ten-pointer any time I wanted to. The trick is to catch them outside the city limits during open season. I'll tell you another thing—you can shoot a hundred-forty pound antelope on my uncle's ranch any time you take a notion."

He gave me a look of extreme skepticism. "Come on, Mr. Oberstdorf, antelopes don't get that big."

"Not if all they get to eat is sagebrush and bunch grass up on the mesas. But antelope that get down into the Deerhorn Valley to feed on hay and grain a few times a week grow really monstrous."

Steve joined me in a drink, pouring himself a cup of coffee from an electric coffee maker that sat on one end of the back bar.

"Tell you what," I said. "Just to prove a point, you come on out to Hessberg next month, and I'll take you hunting. What kind of rifle do you use?"

"A Savage thirty-oh-six bolt action, with a four-power scope. It will down an antelope or deer at twelve hundred yards."

"That far?"

He grinned. "Well, would you settle for a thousand yards? Where is your uncle's place?"

"Which uncle? I have eighty or ninety."

"Uh, the one where the hundred-forty-pound antelopes play."

"Oh, that uncle! He's seven miles north and four west of town, right up on the mesa. My other uncle, my mother's youngest brother, owns a couple of sections in the Deerhorn Valley out south of town. If he hasn't got three or four ten-pointers on his farm, I'll kiss your butt at Sixteenth and Leavenworth at noon on the Fourth of July."

"Mule or white-tail?"

"Either one. Just flip a coin, Mr. Kavich."

A drunk stumbled down into the room from the

stairwell and lurched up to the bar, and Kavich, motioning upward with a thumb, growled, "Hit the road, rummy!"

"You can't turn a man down because of race, creed or color," the man replied, drawing himself up to present a dignified posture. "It ain't constitutional."

"Get out of here, you bum. I'm tired of having you come in here to bug me after you spend your money getting drunk someplace else. Go bug the gink that got you drunk!"

"He shut me off, so he can go to hell. I'll never darken his door again." Hanging onto the bar to prevent falling down, the drunk began beating on the counter heavily with the flat of one hand, demanding a drink, shouting obscenities.

Sliding toward the derelict, surprisingly quick for a man of his bulk, Kavich swung at him brutally with a wet bar towel folded lengthwise. It hit the man with a thwack across one side of his stubbled face, and left a livid welt visible even in the twilight of the basement room. More from surprise than from the blow, he fell to the tile floor, and began crawling frantically toward the stairs. And Steve, angry and violent, ran up behind the crawling man, to kick his butt and send him sprawling into the steps.

While the brutalized drunk clambered out of his predicament, crawling painfully from step to step toward the upper level, the barman returned, complaining bitterly about drunks and vagrants. He cooled off after a time and returned to our conversation about hunting. When he refilled my glass, muttering, "On the house," I knew that I had him hooked. No bartender sets up the second drink unless he expects something in return.

Almost too casually, he asked, "You a friend of Petillo's?"

"Not really," I lied. "I went to the station for help in locating friends or relatives of Keelan. We have him on a slab in Hessberg, and if we can't find somebody to pay for his funeral, the county will have to bury him. There is some indication that he has relatives in Deerhorn County, but they won't come forward. You know how it is when you ask relatives for anything. In this case, his relatives might not want their friends and neighbors to know that they are related to an ex-convict. Some people are so damn narrow-minded. I figure that some of his relatives from up there may have been down to see him lately, to invite him to go hunting or something. There was a rifle in his car when he died." Boy, that was really pouring it on. Maybe I missed my calling; maybe I should have been a fiction writer.

"How was he killed?" Kavich asked. "You guys keep telling me the man is dead, and I read it in the *Star*, but nobody ever says what happened, only that he was found dead in his car."

I shrugged. "Heck, no mystery. He crashed into a brick building during a blizzard. His rig slid out of control right on the main drag in the middle of the afternoon. Snow was blowing so hard that you couldn't see ten feet ahead."

"Oh," he grunted, seeming relieved, "I thought somebody might have shot him or something. Listen, Mr. Oberstdorf, the antelope season opens in two weeks, and the deer season a week later. Do you suppose I could get out onto your uncle's ranch for a day or two?"

"Well, I could talk to him about it."

"Okay," he said, leaning toward me, glancing suspiciously at the snooker players and the other customer, who sat on a stool near the door. "Here it is. I didn't get the guy's name, but Brian was in here a month or so ago with a gink that I never saw before. He was about sixty, gray hair, six-feet tall, and one seventy-five, give or take five pounds. The man wore a tan cowboy hat and a leather, fingertip coat. They sat in a booth over there in the corner." He motioned at a spot beyond the pool table. "But I saw the guy's hair because he took his hat off and laid it on the seat of the booth, and his hair was nearly white. Brian came to the bar for their drinks, so I didn't get a good look at the man's face, but he was as tall as Brian and not as heavy."

"Do you remember what he drank?"

He laughed shortly, more like a snort. "Do I remember what he drank? How could I forget? How many people drink Cutty Sark in milk?"

"Thanks a bundle," I told him. "You just bought yourself a ten-point buck and a hundred-forty-pound pronghorn. Call me a couple of days before you plan to come up. Here's my card—if you can't get me at the office, call me at home."

Glancing at the card, Steve Kavich chuckled. "Is that your real name? I thought you made it up."

"Who would make up a name like *that*?" I asked. "If I wanted to do that, I'd pick something with class—like Steve Kavich."

By then he was laughing all out, happy at my little joke, perhaps, but most happy about the promised hunting on my uncle's nonexistent ranch. I have a paternal uncle and maternal uncle living. One is in a nursing home in Dresden, the other living with his wife in a retirement village in Texas. Had old

Stephan known, he might not have been so happy.
On the other hand, I have a lot of friends and relatives out in the boondocks, and I fully meant to
honor my promise. Why not? The man had virtually
solved my case for me.

"By the way," I said. "I'm looking for a lively
joint that serves a good steak and imported beer—
maybe a slightly risqué floor show."

"Boy, you small-town guys really know how to
live, don't you?" Steve asked.

"Well, yes, I guess so. Just because we're small
town, we're not necessarily small-time. I'll blow
seven or eight dollars if I can have some fun." And
that's what I was doing, having some fun, trying to
be clever, and wasting words sounding like a talking parrot. So, I clammed up, determined to finish
my drink and get out of the place, which was beginning to depress me.

Putting a fresh drink up on the bar for me, Steve
began giving me directions to a lively place with a
good steak, imported beer and a matinee floor
show. He promised that the comedian was better
than Don Rickles and the girl singer cuter than
Marie Osmond.

"What about the risqué stuff?" I asked.

"There ain't none, Felix. Your friend, Petillo, has
closed them all down."

Miss Elvira Whinny came in then, sat at one end
of the bar, and ordered a whiskey coke. While she
sipped at it, I sat looking into the back-bar mirror at
the snooker players, who were hardly more than
dark shadows floating on the perimeter of brightly
lighted table. Dropping my eyes, I studied the blue-
steel automatic pistol that rested on a folded, white
towel beside the cash register. Both towel and pis-

tol were spotlessly clean, which was more than I could say for the rest of the place. Even Steve's beloved trophies—the mounted heads of deer, antelope, coyotes and bobcats—were dusty. The stuffed birds—the grouse, turkeys and pheasants—seemed to be molting.

Miss Whinny had twisted slightly to view the players at the table, and shortly, one of them came to the bar for a round of beers. Ellie eyed him boldly in a manner calculated to provoke interest, and he responded by offering to buy her a drink. Accepting the drink she carried it to a side booth near the pool table, where she sat, oohing and aahing, as the men sank balls into the pockets of the table.

Steve gave her a disgusted look, and told me, "That little bimbo could shoot both them yahoos under the table."

"Oh," I said, pretending to be surprised, "is she a pool hustler?"

"Nah, just a hustler."

Whenever the darker of the men finished a shot, he went over to the booth to have a few words with Elvira and take a drink from his beer bottle, which he let sit on her table. When the game was over, he bought another round before starting a new game, and halfway through the game, Ellie finished her highball and left to climb the stairs quickly, swinging her hips from side to side as she went. When the game was over, the lighter man came to the bar, while the darker one went up the steps. My guess was that he would go through the lobby, and down the hall to room 33. More power to them. For myself, I was feeling good, having, to my own satisfaction, solved the Heffner case. All I had to do before going to the place that had good steaks and import-

ed beer was call Red to thank him for his help, and
find a sculptor to do the Schweitzer for Milly.

Calling Steve Kavich, I asked him where I could
find a sculptor. He didn't know, but the snooker
player did. That may surprise you, but it didn't surprise me. Any time you sit in a saloon with three
sophisticated men of the world, and between them,
they do not know all the answers, then you are in
the wrong establishment.

**9**

THERE IS A TENDENCY to assume that while we are
gone, nothing happens, whether we are gone for a
day or for a year. It is probably because each of us is
the very center of his own tiny world and feels subconsciously that the little world stops spinning
when he is not in it. Upon sober reflection, we see
that this is not so, that things happen whether we
are there to see them or not. As an example of this,
a lot of things happened in Hessberg the day I was
in Win City. For one thing, another dead body
turned up, this time in the ashes of the elevator
fire. For another thing, Louis Post refused to take
an A.F.D.C. application. As you may know, this
was formerly called Aid To Dependent Children,
commonly referred to as A.D.C. In recent years,
some bright person in some federal agency came up
with the idea that aid to children is really aid to the
families of dependent children. That is probably so,
and if it justifies the salary of some political hack in
some obscure office of the federal bureaucracy, so
be it. The third significant event that transpired
during my absence was the withdrawal by the Wolf
family of their applications for assistance. To make
it more puzzling, Charlie entered Sisters' Hospital in
Neu Koblenz to have his hernia repaired—at his
own expense.

The first item that I had to deal with was the application of Charmaine Schelhase for help, after my peerless young caseworker had refused to take her application. Had Mr. Post been more familiar with the Schelhase clan of Willow Creek, he might not have been so hasty. It is good to act with caution in denying them anything, especially something that is legally theirs to claim. The Schelhase family is a Tobacco Road type group from a remote settlement in the West River district. They are poor, dirty, mean and numerous. If I had to choose an enemy, you can bet that it would not be one of them. Because for one thing, they are like a hive of hornets. You get one of them after you, and the entire clan comes whining, diving, stinging in a rage.

Living in a scattering of shacks along Willow Creek in Butte Township, the family comprises the entire town of Willow Creek, which is not really a town, but a place. You may recall a ditty that Phil Harris used to sing: "Doo-wah ditty, it ain't no town, it ain't no city." Willow Creek fits that song to a tee. They earn a precarious living poaching deer, antelope and elk—trapping fur animals, in and out of season and mooching. In time of great emergency they will work, but that is a very rare occurrence. They are wise to the ways of welfare, and in fact, derive a fair share of their annual income from our agency and others. Maude Schelhase, Charmaine's skinny, hollow-chested mother, knows more about the technicalities of public assistance than do most of the people who work in public agencies.

Maude, her hulking husband, Arnie Wolfgang Schelhase, Charmie and her new baby, along with Bobby Schelhase, were waiting for me in the outer office when I went in to work Friday morning. Charmaine's elder brother, Bobby, is six feet five inches tall, even stooping, as is his habit. He is always scowling, and always needs a shave. There is an ugly cyst high on his right cheek, surrounded by a field of blackheads, and he hasn't had a shampoo, much less a haircut, in three or four years.

"Come on in," I invited them, going into my office to find sanctuary behind my big desk. "To what do I owe the honor of this visit?"

"We got cut off welfare," Maude whined.

"Not yet," I said.

Without waiting for an invitation, the entire group sat down on a row of chairs in front of my desk, to stare at me accusingly.

"Where is that miserable little squat-to-pee that you sent out to see my sister?" Bobby demanded. "I have got a good mind to spank his butt!"

"Take it easy, son," Arnie cautioned. "Don't get all riled up. All we want to do is get Charmie and the baby on welfare."

"And me," Maude said, looking like an angry, ruffle-feathered stork sitting on the wood of the chair.

"*You?*" I asked.

"Yes, me. I've been in poor health for over a year—asthma and short breath, and all that. My heart ain't what it used to be, either. I tell you, Mr. Oberstdorf, you bring seven children into this world and raise them up, and it takes something out of you."

"Are you planning to apply for Aid To The Disabled?" I asked her fearfully.

"Yessir," she replied. "Section 36, Paragraph 16-A, Revised Statutes of 1957."

Oh, boy! For some time, I had been looking forward to the day when Charmaine would be eighteen, and no longer a dependent for A.F.D.C. Now, it looked as if we might add a case instead of dropping one. Arnie, who had a mouthful of chewing tobacco, was slobbering, and looking around for someplace to spit, and I told him to go out my hall door and spit in the men's can across the corridor. Waiting for him to return, I asked Bobby how he would like to make an easy twenty bucks.

"What do I have to do?" he asked, suspicion showing in his weathered face.

"I have a friend in Win City who wants to shoot a really big pronghorn. If you can show him one, I'll give you twenty dollars out of my own pocket. If he wants a ten-point buck, he will have to pay for that himself."

He laughed shortly. "Heck, for twenty dollars I'll show him where to shoot an Angus steer."

"Your own, I hope."

"You kidding?" he scoffed, showing yellow fangs in a wolfish grin. Then, seriously he said, "Bring him out, Mr. O. If I don't show him at least a hundred-thirty pound antelope, it won't cost you a dime."

"What about the ten-point buck?"

"For another twenty, I'll show him a ten-pointer," he promised, "but I won't guarantee that he'll kill it. All I can do is show him where it is. The rest is up to him."

When Arnie returned, buttoning his fly, I asked them, "Now, what is this about being refused an application?"

Charmie, who had been sullen, began to pout heavily. "He wouldn't take my application," she complained, "because I won't name the father of my baby." Her lower lip quivered.

"Why not?" I asked. "Is it a secret?"

"It ain't no secret," she replied, stealing a glance at her big brother, "I just don't know."

"Charmie is a very popular girl," Arnie explained, looking down at me from his height. "She has got a lot of boyfriends." If old Arnie is not quite as tall as Bobby, he is every bit as unkempt, and is twice as ugly.

"I hope it was that nice boy that used to work for Mr. Miegs," Maude told me. "He was such a handsome boy. We don't want no ugly babies in our house."

"I think it was Ronnie Bird Song, mama," the girl said hopefully.

"Nah, that kid don't look like no Indian," Arnie said, leaning over to stare at the baby, a blue-eyed blond wrapped in a soiled bath towel.

Taking two application forms out of my desk, I called Sara in and told her to take Maude's application for A.D. and Charmaine's application for A.F.D.C., then I charged through the outer office, past the secretaries pecking half-heartedly at their typewriters, into the caseworkers' office, glad that Fanny wasn't in.

Without preamble I asked Louis, "Why the hell did you refuse to take that girl's application for assistance?"

Startled, he hesitated momentarily before answering. "Well, she refused to name the father."

"That's none of your business, you pompous, half-assed little fop," I told him savagely. "Who the hell is running this office—you or me?"

"I thought they had to name the father," he said weakly.

"You know better than that," I told him, beginning to regain control of my anger. "You are an M.S.W. It took you six years of college to get so smart, and you know the manual by heart, or should. Jesus Christ, do I have to follow you all over the county to keep you from starving people to death?"

He began to get back his arrogance. "They won't starve—they steal."

"Just a minute," I said, and stepping to the door, I barked at pimply Linda, "Get Bobby Schelhase over here, Linda—right now!"

The girl leaped out of her chair to rush into my office, and seconds later Bobby was with us, towering menacingly.

"Bobby," I said softly, "do you steal?"

He glowered. "Do I what?"

"Do you *steal*—you know, take things that don't belong to you?"

"Did this little punk say that?" He stepped toward Louis, who shrank back.

"Oh, no," I said hastily, "Louis wouldn't say a thing like that. Would you, Mr. Post?"

"Of course not," he said fearfully, eyeing the big animal that towered above him so menacingly.

"You tell me who said that, Mr. O., and I'll break his back in five places."

"Nobody said it," I said, "we just heard it. Thanks for coming in, Bobby. Mr. Post is going to see that your family gets good service from now on. Aren't you, Mr. Post?"

"Yes," the caseworker muttered, huddling behind his desk for protection.

Giving Bobby time to get out of the room, I told Louis, "One should never traffic in rumor and gossip. And another thing, buddy—you had better learn who is running this office."

"I have never questioned that!" he cried.

"Not directly you haven't, but you have in a hundred little, snide ways. You think that because you are from the city and sat in class long enough on federal grants to get a higher degree, you are somehow a superior person. Let me be honest with you, Louis, Fanny Brodus is a better caseworker than you'll ever be, and all she has is a mere bachelor's degree from Valley Tech. More than that, my secretary is a better social worker than you are, and she is only a high-school graduate. If you would resign, it might take me three or four days to replace you."

"You can't fire me," he said sullenly, not looking me in the eye.

"Maybe I can and maybe I can't," I told him, "but what I *can* do is make life so miserable for you that you'll be glad to resign. For starters, Louis, don't ever come in two minutes late from now on, and don't take off sick without following the rules to the tee—see a doctor before you return. Don't sluff off on private business some afternoon when things are a little slow. Don't you dare go one inch outside Kornfeld County during the workday. That means you don't slip over to Neu for a matinee or down to Win City to see your mother. I'm on to all your little dodges, and I'll be watching you very closely from now on."

When it was over, I felt a lot better, because I had been putting it off for a long time, letting the young guy wear me down with his insolence and arrogance. Once it was done, I felt proud of myself and sorry for him, but only momentarily. It was too easy for me to recall the dozens, scores, hundreds of smart remarks, sly grins, and superior, patronizing statements that the man had pushed my way for six months. Had he sat down and written out his resignation, I'd have accepted it gladly. But he didn't, because he is like so many of the new generation—plenty of gall, but no guts. If a boss had talked to me like that when I was a young man, I'd have hit him in the mouth, or at least quit the job.

After ushering the Schelhase family out of my office, I walked over to the mortuary to have a look at our latest dead stranger, stopping at the hotel coffee shop for a piece of pie and a cup of coffee. Sissy was on duty and had a big, country-girl smile for me. I tipped her a quarter, and promised her once more that my son Heinie would look her up during Christmas vacation. Miss Borchers, if you are curious, is twenty-one years old, a graduate of Central Junior College, and the only child of the folks who own the hotel. Instead of running off to the city, Sissy chose to stay in Hessberg and learn the food and lodging business from the ground up, if you will pardon a mild pun. And yes, she is a granddaughter of Klaus, and thus a first cousin of Frankie.

Clancy Depew, who was having coffee and rolls at the hotel with Snooks Hunter and Boney Hartmann, hailed me to their booth as I got up from my stool at the lunch counter. So I sat down and got suckered into their conversation. Anyway, I wanted to have a word with Clancy about our mutual friends lying in state in his parlor at the funeral home.

"Hey, there," Snooks chortled, bobbing his Adam's apple down in his long neck. "Where the heck have you been, Felix? Did you know that they found a bullet in the post office yesterday? I *thought* I heard shots that night the gangster was killed.''

"He wasn't killed," I said, "he died in an accident. And what makes you think he was a gangster? Who found the bullet?"

They all tried to answer me at the same time, but Boney got there first. "The postmaster, of course. Who else? Found it Wednesday when he was sweeping up. It came through a corner of the window, way up high, where nobody would ever think to look—knocked out a chunk of glass the size of a quarter. Norbie spotted the glass on the floor and got to looking up at the window. Then he got a stepladder from the basement and climbed up to investigate the hole in the glass. That's when he saw the spot on the casing—"

"And," I said, "he went downstairs to get a screwdriver, and dug the bullet out of the wood."

Boney was surprised. "How did you know that, Obie?"

"Oh, just a stab in the dark," I replied, winking at Clancy.

Boney, like Snooks, is a relic of the day when everybody had a nickname. When the thinnest kid in town was Skinny, and the fattest one Fatty or Fats. Every small town had its Swede, who was not necessarily Swedish, but was always blond. There was a Satch or Satchel, shortened from satchel ass, and Red, whose hair was some shade of red. If you were dark, you automatically became either Nig or Blackie, and short guys were Shorty. Strangely, if you were very tall and heavy, you were not Biggie, but Tiny. Deaf people were Dummy, and people with mental problems, Crazy.

In this one phase of society at least, we are getting more civilized. It is not only cruel, but unnecessary to demean a person by drawing attention to him or her, to label a person in such fashion. To be different from one's fellows is bad enough, without having that difference put on display.

"It was a forty-five caliber," said Boney, who as a boy was so skinny that his bones showed.

"This town is no longer safe," Snooks told us solemnly, "for a citizen to walk the streets, tending his own business. Why, there have been three brutal murders in less than two weeks!"

"Murders?" I asked, raising my brows.

"Yes, three—Barney was killed."

"Was he?"

"Keelan was killed."

"Are you sure?"

"And this latest one was killed," Snooks finished. In case you are squirming with curiosity, I'll tell you where Snooks got his nickname. When he was taking his barber training in Omaha on the G.I. bill after World War II, he played a lot of snooker in a pool hall next door to the barber college. He got to be pretty good, and when he came home after his training, he used to play snooker with traveling condom salesmen in the pool hall on Thirteenth and Prairie. We began calling him Snooker. It was eventually shortened to Snooks, and it stuck. That is another thing about nicknames; sometimes they stick, sometimes they don't. Snooks's real name is Hannibal Scipio Hunter. Chances are that he would rather be called Snooks than Hanna.

"Who is the latest corpse?" I asked, looking at the undertaker, who is a short, greasy man, built like a mud turtle.

He threw up his hands in a helpless gesture. "Who knows? Ab Collins got his prints and sent them to the state office."

"I'd think his prints would have been burned off in the fire."

"They would have been, but he was wearing asbestos gloves—the kind you wear at outdoor steak fries. His face and body were burned black, like charcoal."

"Could he be a local man?"

"Nobody is missing," Depew replied. "At least not that we know of. Local officials have not had any requests to look for a missing person."

Snooks butted in. "It's open and shut, guys. Somebody hired the arsonist to come up here and burn Brownie out. Then, when the fire was raging, the person who hired him hit him on the head and threw him into the fire."

"What for?" I asked him.

He gawked at me. "What for *what*? What for the man was hired to burn the elevator, or what for his employer killed him?"

"Both."

The barber thought about it for a long time, marshaling his thoughts, then said, "Okay, somebody had it in for Braunholz and wanted to get him. That is the *what for* of the arson. Then, the person who hired the arsonist killed him to keep him quiet. That is the *what for* of the killing. Listen, I have to get back to the shop. I left a sign on the door saying I'd be back in twenty minutes, and that was forty minutes ago." He held one arm up to get a look at his wristwatch. "Forty-three minutes, in fact."

"Before you leave," I said, "tell me one thing."

He paused halfway out of his seat. "What's that?"

"How do you know the man was killed?"

"Elementary, dear Watson. His skull was caved in." And he squeezed past Boney and went toward the door.

"The man got a good crack on the noggin," Depew told me. "He has a bad fracture."

"Couldn't he have been thrown against a wall of the elevator by the explosion? That might have cracked his head open."

"What explosion? I didn't know there was an explosion."

Our conversation went on like that for another fifteen minutes, with Hartmann chiming in from time to time, and I learned that there was to be a town-hall meeting Saturday night to discuss the alleged murders. From what the two men told me, Hessberg was on the verge of panic following the third death. And only a week earlier, virtually everybody in town had been poking fun at me about my concern over Barney's death.

When the funeral director had finished his rolls and a third cup of coffee, we went over to his place of business, and I got a look at the body and agreed to pay for a county burial.

"The damned county really should pay me more than a lousy two hundred dollars," Clancy complained, "to bury these stiffs. Don't you think so, Obie?"

"I do, but the supervisors don't, Clancy." That was a bare-faced lie, but there was no point in arguing with him. He would never be convinced, and arguing would only alienate him for no purpose. Anyway, it was a little white lie, intended to make him feel better. The truth is, in my opinion, that two hundred dollars is enough, maybe too much. The coffin is a thin, yellow-pine box, covered with about five dollars worth of printed cotton. The hole is dug in a few minutes, using a power digger hooked up to a jeep. The whole thing shouldn't really cost more than fifty dollars.

No funeral should cost more than that. We all return to the organic materials, the chemicals that we are composed of, anyway, whether the funeral costs two hundred dollars or two hundred thousand. The main thing is that loving survivors often feel guilty about how rotten they treated the dead ones while they were living, and they try to make amends with a jazzy funeral. Or, if not that, some relative likes to put on the dog, to show people in the community what a real, class funeral is like. After all, isn't that what the insurance money is for?

Clancy Depew, like most small-town morticians, has a half dozen models on display in his shop, running from the cheap, yellow-pine and printed-cloth item, to a lavish aluminum vault, with brass carrying handles and a price tag of five thousand dollars, plus tax. He has a walnut and copper box, a precast cement box, with decals of flying angels on it, and a lovely bronze casket, polished to a dark glow. These, and a sturdy oak box fastened together with gold-plated screws, comprise his entire display, but in addition, he has a picture catalog of many other models, available on twenty-four hours' notice from a wholesale house in Denver. So, old Clancy is well equipped to handle any funeral that comes up, whether simple or grandiose. He is right on Prairie Avenue, in a mansion with a columned facade. It sits back from the street on a double lot shaded by towering hackberry trees. A ribbon of cement curves into the mortuary and under the portico. In addition to the building, caskets, and his tools and pumps, Depew has a hearse and a limousine, both Cadillacs, both shiny black, and both quite elderly. These big rigs, costing a lot of money when new, are factors in the price of a funeral. In my opinion, there is no reason at all why a corpse should not be hauled away in a pickup truck and the pallbearers taken along in a station wagon, if at all.

Looking at the charred body nearly made me sick, and it was getting on toward lunchtime. This is one of the little unpleasantries that balance somewhat the many joys of being a welfare director in a place like Hessberg. Fleeing the depression of the funeral parlor, I used a telephone in the outer lobby to call Sara and tell her that I'd be out the rest of the morning, and I went home to get my car and drive down to have a look at the burned elevator. It was more than a mile from home, and not a pleasant walk in the thaw of another bright day that had water running in the streets. The snow had been melting for three days, but not at night. With sunset, the temperatures went below freezing, the melting stopped, and water, which nearly ran over the banks of the creek during the day, ran off into the Deerhorn. By morning the level was down to normal, allowing for the flood of a daytime thaw. At the rate it was melting, I figured the snow to be all gone by Sunday night without any danger of flooding.

Railroad Avenue, which runs due east from the
river, is in effect the southern boundary of town,
although there are a few houses sprinkled around
on the hillside south of the avenue. Driving south
on Fourteenth, I hit Railroad, and wheeled west
toward the railroad track and the Braunholz mills,
which lie just east of the river and south of the
avenue. Potholes in the road were filled with dirty
water that splashed up against the sides of my car,
causing me to curse out loud.

Jack's house, a profane example of Roaring
Twenties architecture, crouches on a bluff looking
out over his business. From his living room he can
watch not only the elevator, but anything that
comes up or down the Deerhorn Valley. The railroad, which runs from Winnebago City to the Blue
Hills along the east bank of the river, has a spur running up to the elevator and beyond to community
loading pens, where cattle and sheep have been
loaded and unloaded for generations. They are at
Seventh and Railroad Avenue, and there are usually a few head of range cattle milling around in the
pens, waiting to be picked up by one of the many
feeders in our area. By virtue of geography, the
Deerhorn Valley is a prime feeder region, being at a
place where in agricultural terms East meets West.
It is here that our great cattle ranches end and our
grain farms begin. And as it is cheaper to haul range
cattle to the feedlots and the packing plants than to
take the grain and packing facilities west, that's
where the feedlots are—at the western edge of the
grain belt. In fact, the Braunholz elevators are really too far west in the grain belt, but are in the rich
valley and on the railroad, enabling them to get
grain for storage. There was indeed a necessity for

storage in the area when Jack came to town many years ago with his proposition for the community.

Jack and a stranger were viewing the ruins when I drove up, and he gave me a wave and a smile. The other man, wearing a plaid jacket, corduroy pants, and rubber boots, was making notes on a lined pad as he walked, nodding and pursing his lips.

When I got out of my car and walked up to them, Jack said, "Hi, there, Felix. I suppose you came down to see the remains of the fire."

"Not just for that," I told him. "The county is faced with paying for the burial of the man who was doing the arson. I thought you might have some idea as to who he is." Looking over the smoldering ruins, sniffing of the stench that emanated from mounds of partially burned corn that littered the siding, I said, "Wow, that was a real humdinger of a fire, wasn't it?"

"It sure was, Felix." He gave me a sincere stare, and shook his head slowly. "No, I haven't got an idea in the world who the man is. All my men are accounted for."

"That brings up another question," I said. "Are you going to let some of them go now?"

"Oh, no, I'll spread them around, Felix. I lose two or three a month anyway, by natural attrition. It's too close to Christmas to let anybody go."

Don't put on your Santa Claus act for me, you phony-baloney, I thought, but didn't say anything.

The stranger, who was looking at me with some interest, said, "That must have been some kind of storm to blow all that corn away like that."

"It certainly was," I assured him.

Braunholz introduced us. "Mr. Hawkins, this is our county welfare director, Felix Oberstdorf—Jim

Hawkins, Felix, from the Department of Agriculture."

Sticking his pen behind an ear, the federal man put out a hand, saying, "Pleased to meet you, sir."

Taking the hand, I gave it a couple of pumps and said, "Yessir, welcome to Hessberg."

We went to within twenty feet of the great silo, which had been blown open at the top, and had a gaping hole at ground level.

"The way I figure it," Jack boomed, "the combustion must have blowed the hole in the bottom. That let in enough oxygen to get the fire going good, and it melted the top out. Then, the updraft just sucked out all the burning grain and the wind blew it away."

How convenient, I thought.

"I suppose," suggested Hawkins, "that the corn is covered with snow, and will be washed into the river when the snow thaws." It was hard to read any meaning into the words or to interpret the steady gaze of his hazel eyes.

The big elevator man grunted, and shrugged massive shoulders. "I guess so. There should be a lot of fat catfish in the river come spring." He laughed nervously, and Hawkins gave him an appraising glance.

I kept the pot boiling. "Do you suppose that the dead man was a drifter, just passing through?"

"Could be," Jack replied, seeming to like the idea. "He could have been a hobo who dropped off a train and sneaked into the elevator to get warm. You can pull a little door at the bottom, and pull out enough grain to make room for a nap. We've had it happen in the past. Why, I remember one cold winter when we had to evict thirty or forty bums

out of the elevators. Maybe the guy lighted a ciga-
rette and exploded the collected dust in there.''

"That theory is all right, except for one thing,
Jack.''

He stared at me, having trouble to grasp my
meaning. Apparently, nobody had told him about
the asbestos gloves. "Yeah? What's that, Felix?''

"The man," I told him, "was wearing asbestos
gloves. That guy was an arsonist, Jack. Somebody
paid him to burn your elevator. He might have been
a drifter, maybe even a hobo, but he set fire to the
grain silo.''

Braunholz appeared to be stunned. "Who would
do a thing like that, Felix?'' He turned wounded
eyes upon Hawkins. "Who would hate me that
much—try to ruin me financially? My God, the insurance won't cover half of my loss, and you know
what it would cost to replace this structure.''

Maybe Uncle Sam will give you the money, I
thought, like before. But I said, "We all have
enemies, Jack—sick ones, envious ones, vicious
ones, that we don't always know about. Look at
Barney Heffner. Would you believe that somebody
hated him enough to have him killed?''

"I haven't got any enemies like that," Jack said.

"Okay," I said, winking at Hawkins, "maybe one
of your friends did it. With a friend like that, you
don't *need* any enemies. Seriously, Jack, you probably have a couple of enemies. Even Jesus Christ had
some. You are a successful, prominent man. There
are bound to be people who envy, even despise you,
for your wealth.''

I noted that his bald head was sweating in the
sun, and that his shirt was wet under the arms. Although the day was warm for November, it was not

too warm for a jacket, but Jack was not wearing one.

"That's right," Hawkins put in. "Some people hate anybody who has more than they have themselves."

Big John began to look more comfortable, almost smug. "By golly," he said, looking from one to another of us, "you fellows may be right. Hey, come on, let's go get a cup of coffee." He led us into his private office, an ancient but solid railway coach that sat on an unused sidetrack, a hundred yards from the elevators. The car, bought at an auction in 1964, was in mint condition, having been restored as of 1900, when it was the rolling palace of a railroad baron. Walking into it was like taking a trip into the past in all its elegance, all its mahogany, velvet drapery, and all its porcelain of another era. A jarring note was the Silex coffeepot that he kept hot at all times on an electric heating coil.

"Sugar and cream?" he asked, reaching for the pot with one hand and cups with the other.

"Coal black," I said.

"A dash of cream," Hawkins told him, gazing about the car in appreciation. "Man, this is really *something*!"

Old Jack began to puff up, and I told Hawkins, "President Hayes slept here."

"Did he?" Jim Hawkins did not know whether I was kidding or not. Sipping his coffee, he watched my face for a sign.

I admitted that I was kidding, but added that it could have been so, because Hayes was still living when the car was built. And that was no lie.

"He *probably* did," Jack added, "and maybe some other presidents did, too."

Then I asked Jim whether he planned to stay in town for the meeting on Saturday night. He asked what meeting, and I told him about the proposed meeting to discuss the recent acts of violence in our community.

"If you will pardon my saying so, Mr. Oberstdorf, it seems to me that the town is unduly upset over an unfortunate series of accidents. These things happen every day, all over the country."

"But not in Hessberg," I replied. "Besides that, two of the deaths look like murder, and the other may be related to them."

"Oh, in what way?"

"Well, the man who died in the crash is suspected of killing the man who died on the fence."

"And?"

"And the man who died in the fire died the same day that the other man died in the auto accident. They may have come into town together."

"How's that?" Jack asked, arching his shaggy brows.

"Keelan," I explained, "was a convicted felon, out on parole. If the man burned to death in the fire was a professional arsonist, chances are that they knew each other. They may even have been working together on something."

"What?"

I admitted that I didn't know, but that I meant to find out.

Jim Hawkins stared at me, thinking hard. "What possible connection could there be in these deaths?"

"That," I told him, "is the sixty-four dollar question. If I knew that, the case would be solved, but it could be that the person who wanted Barney Heffner out of the way wanted Jack's corn out of the way.''

Jack and Jim looked at each other, seeming to ask each other about my sanity, but I was getting used to that kind of reaction, so it didn't bother me.

Pouring himself another cup of the mouth-tingling coffee, the federal agent knit his brow in deep thought. Finally he came out of it to ask me, ''What was violent about Keelan's death? I thought it was an accident.''

''It was, but he was trying to run over me when it happened.''

''Next question,'' Braunholz said. ''Why was he after *you*, Felix?''

''Maybe because I was getting close to him. I knew who he was and what kind of car he drove and that he had been watching the Heffner place before Barney was killed.''

''Very interesting. How did you know all that?''

''Easy. Old Man Miller gave me the license number, and Abner Collins, a state policeman, ran a check on the owner of the car.''

''Do you know who the other dead man is?''

''Not yet, but Collins sent his prints to Win City. We should have an ID in a day or so. If I'm not mistaken, we are going to find out that he and Keelan were associates.''

Seeming concerned and thoughtful, the big grain man fell silent. Looking out the car window at his empire, he began to bite at his bottom lip.

Out in the yard, there was a steady whine and roar of heavy trucks hauling grain away from the elevators, and I heard the faint cries of workmen yelling instructions at each other. It was eleven-thirty, nearly lunchtime for me. Putting my empty

cup onto a tray beside the coffeepot, I excused myself and stepped out of the nineteenth century into
a twentieth-century day of dazzling sunlight and
mushy railroad siding. Walking warily, from dry
spot to dry spot, I mentally added a few more pieces
to my jigsaw puzzle of murder. The pieces were falling into place with increasing speed and ease.

**10**

THERE ARE TWO HIGHWAYS from Hessberg to Neu Koblenz, our regional trading center. Interstate 90 follows the river in a great figure S southeast to the Mormon Crossing, then northeast to Neu. At Neu, it turns with the river, southeast toward Win City. It is not the most direct route to Neu Koblenz, but is the fastest as you don't have to slow down or stop anyplace. The road bypasses towns and there are no cross roads, only cloverleaf entries. Eighty-seven, on the other hand, is a direct route, running straight east, but goes through several small towns that have stop signs and speed limits. In addition to that, the country between the two towns is mostly rolling hills, so that the road goes up and down most of the way, like a roller coaster with eighteen miles of tracks. We usually go one way and come back the other, to avoid so much monotony.

Ellen likes to get into Neu two or three times a month if she can, to shop and visit with relatives. It's her hometown, and she has a sister there, as well as numerous cousins and former classmates. For that matter, I enjoy the trip myself, as Neu is a dozen or fifteen times the size of Hessberg and has considerably more to offer in the way of shopping and entertainment. They have a Sears-Roebuck, a J.C. Penney and a Montgomery-Ward, several drug

stores and eating houses, and more saloons than
you could cover in a week. There is even a Holiday
Inn with a domed courtyard and swimming pool.
You can sit out there in the dead of winter in your
shirt-sleeves, eating, drinking or just loafing, while
people splash in the pool. There are little lemon
trees and palmettos growing among various kinds of
flowers and shrubs, all potted and carefully tended.
There are several district offices of state government, including welfare, vocational rehabilitation,
highways and state police. The town is, in fact, the
unofficial capital of the north central part of the
state, with a trade territory encompassing twenty
thousand square miles. That includes the vast Cedar
Ridge Indian reservation, whose southern boundary
is the northern boundary of Deerhorn County. In
addition to a fifty-thousand watt radio station,
there is a daily newspaper with a paid circulation of
more than twenty-five thousand, and a television
relay station. So, communication is pretty good,
and it is a place where you can do anything that you
are big enough to do. Aside from that, Neu is almost
as much a hometown to me as is Hessberg. It was
there that I met my wife, while working as a caseworker in the Deerhorn County welfare office. She
was then a starry-eyed young school teacher, Ellen
Elizabeth Schmidt, a dreamer and poet. How the
years affect our interests. When we were going
together, she used to read to me from Byron and
Keats, as well as from her own notebooks of verse.
Now she won't even read to me from the letters
that she receives from the boys. We used to sit in
the living room of the Gothic house on Cedar Lane
on Sunday afternoons, when I was lucky enough to
be invited to dinner. I was scared stiff of her father,

a gruff barrel of a man who worked most of his life as a printer for the *Neu Koblenz Daily Mail* and its companion newspaper, *Die Koblenzer Zeitung*, a German language weekly. He would try to get me to speak German during these Sunday dinners, and I was so self-conscious, because all the German I knew was a smidgin picked up in high school and college. It always seemed to me that Henry Schmidt looked down on me because my father's family was Austrian and Catholic. There was always an unspoken indication that Austrian was not quite German and that Catholic was not quite Christian. It didn't seem to make any difference to old Heinie that my father spoke better German than he did, or that my mother had managed to get me baptized in the First Lutheran Church of San Diego, California, shortly after I was born, thus saving me from perdition. Despite his difficult ways, I was quite fond of the man, and in fact, named my younger son for him. When he died of lung cancer in 1969, it hit me as hard as it did any of his children.

I dropped Ellen off at the home of her sister, Arlene, at eleven forty-five Saturday morning, and drove up to Sisters' Hospital for a visit with Charlie Wolf, who had survived his hernia operation in great fashion, and was sitting up in bed, reading a mystery novel. From his aloofness, I got the idea that he was not exactly beside himself with joy to see me.

"Oh, hi," he grunted. "Come on in, Felix." He seemed reluctant to put his book down.

"How goes it?" I asked.

"Okay, I guess. The doctor tells me that I'll be going home Wednesday or Thursday."

"Great! How soon can you go back to work?"

"He says two weeks. The boss is going to give me some light work." Charlie did not look at me directly.

A tiny wren of a nun came fluttering in, chirping, "How are we today, Mr. Wolf?" She lifted his chart from its hook at the foot of his bed, gave it a quick reading, then went to the window to adjust his shade.

He grinned. "Fine and dandy, sister. If you wasn't married, I'd jump out of bed and chase you around the room!"

"Aw, you would not," she said, winking at me.

"Don't kid yourself, sister," I told her. "He is an evil man."

"And he knows me better than you do," Charlie added. When the nun left, he cried, "For Christ sake, Felix, please pull that shade down, will you? The damn sun hits me right in the face!" Then, squinting his eyes, he halfway apologized for canceling his welfare application. "I couldn't do it, Felix. I just couldn't go on welfare. So, I went over and had me a talk with old Dieter Emhoff, and he agreed to keep me on the payroll just like I was never hurt."

"Is that the same Dieter Emhoff who got you to sign a paper absolving him of all blame for the accident?" I asked.

"I had a secret weapon," he boasted, reaching for a water glass on his bedstand.

"Very interesting," I said. "Are you going to tell me about it, Charlie?"

"Nope! If I told you, it wouldn't be a secret anymore."

"Does it have something to do with the work that Barney used to perform for Emhoff?"

"Maybe it does and maybe it don't," he replied, smiling mysteriously. "What are you, Felix, some kind of undercover man?"

"No, just a friend of Barney's, Charlie."

"So am I!" he said, leaning forward angrily, staring at me with murky eyes. "But snitching on Dieter Emhoff won't bring Barney back."

"I'm not trying to bring Barney back," I told him. "All I'm trying to do is bring his killer to justice."

"I can't see what that has to do with Emhoff."

"You might be surprised," I replied.

That was the way it went for a half hour, and when I left the hospital, there was another little piece fitted into my jigsaw puzzle.

At the district patrol office, Abner Collins gave me another piece. "The torch was Wilbur Feenan, a former cell mate of Keelan at the pen. His bag is auto theft. Maybe that's why he got himself knocked off starting a fire."

"What do you mean by that?"

Ab fastened his eyes on me. "What I mean is, he was a professional car thief but an amateur arsonist. The man didn't know what he was doing. No professional torch would toss a Molotov Cocktail into a combustible chamber like a grain elevator."

"Did he do that?"

"We don't know, but it is the kind of thing that an amateur would do, and the kind of thing that would result in an explosion. In fact, had his body not been found, the state fire marshal might well have found that the fire was caused by spontaneous combustion. As you know, it is very common in elevators. Feenan probably did what any amateur would do—filled a few plastic jugs with gasoline and oil and tossed them into the silo, then stuffed a rag into another jug to make a Molotov Cocktail. When he threw it into the silo, he ignited not only the other jugs of fuel, but what dust fumes were gathered in there. Keelan may have driven Feenan to the site, helped him place the jugs in the silo, and left Wilbur there to fire them after dark, or whenever he thought it was time. Chances are that they arranged to meet someplace along the road, after the fire was started. But, it all went sour on them, and they both got killed."

"Then," I said, "maybe Keelan bungled the Heffner job, too. Maybe he didn't mean to kill him, just scare him."

"Could be," Abner admitted. "You know Barney. If somebody tried to scare him, he might get angry, even violent. Keelan might have ended up by shooting in self-defense."

Having exhausted the subject of the fire, I told Collins everything that I knew, from start to finish, including details of the coal vein, my trip to Win City, and my recent visit with Charlie Wolf. Naturally, Ab recognized the citizen described by Kavich as having been with Keelan in the Avalon. For while it is true that a lot of people around Hessberg are six feet tall and weigh one-seventy, and a few of them have gray hair and two or three of these wear tan cowboy hats and leather jackets, there is just one man who answers to all those demands and also drinks Scotch whiskey in milk.

"But it's still only circumstantial," Ab told me. "He may have known Keelan, and he may have wanted Barney out of the way, and he may have wanted to burn the elevator. But so far, all you have is a theory."

"I'm going to ask O'Shay to issue a warrant," I insisted.

Abner laughed in my face. "Hell, Felix, that pipsqueak won't do it. He'll find ten thousand reasons not to."

"You are probably right, Ab, but I'm going to ask him, anyway."

"When?"

"Tonight, at the town meeting."

He sighed. "Okay, pardner. I'll be there with bells on. Are you staying in town for lunch?"

"Yeah. My wife is at her sister's place; we'll probably eat there."

We usually eat at Arlene's table when we are in town, but sometimes go to a local restaurant like the Holiday, or the Famous Beef House, or to Sydow's, which puts out a nice meal at a fair price, and has imported beer. If you ever stop in Neu Koblenz, be sure to try Sydow's. You can get a Wiener schnitzel, which is a veal cutlet with sour gravy, or jaeger schnitzel, which is known in some places as Hungarian goulash, and in other places as Irish stew. A rose by any name is as sweet, I suppose. Sydow's serves a nice steak, too, principally because there is such good beef available, but I rarely eat steak when we dine out, because I get so much of it at home. We have a big freezer in our basement, and most of it is filled with choice steaks— round, T-bone, tenderloins, and rump. The way I fry it is in a skillet sizzling with fresh bacon grease. After salting and peppering the meat, I pop it into the hot grease and let it char on one side for a few minutes, then turn it over to char the other side. This seals in the juices and flavor. Then, I fry it medium rare, until the meat is pink, but not bloody. On the side, I like rice with soy sauce and butter, a combination that you don't get in every steak house you walk into. In the summertime, I cook my steaks on an outdoor grill in my backyard, and that is even better. But sometimes while I'm eating, a *Luftwaffe* of giant mosquitoes comes up from the creek to attack me. If things go right, I'm going to put a gazebo up in the backyard. I'll have my grill right in the middle and screen all around.

Anyway, when I left the patrol office, I drove over to get Ellen at Arlene's place, but they were gone, leaving Arlene's husband, Eppie Jarl, to guard the estate. He was in the basement with his Guinea pigs. Eppie, my favorite brother-in-law, refers to the basement as the piggery, and to his little animals as hogs. He does not feed his Guinea pigs, but slops the hogs. He has been in the Guinea pig business two years, during which time he has sold a hundred dollars worth of the hairy beasts to strange people like himself. There are Guinea pigs all over his basement, in cages stacked from floor to ceiling on all four walls. He has brown pigs, black pigs, white pigs, and spotted pigs, rough pigs, smooth pigs, girl pigs, boy pigs, and suckling pigs. Far from getting rich selling Guinea pigs, old Eppie was getting poor feeding them. He was, in fact, feeding them when I walked into the house and started yelling to announce myself.

"Downstairs!" He yelled back. "Slopping the hogs, Obie!"

Going down the steps, trying to keep from laughing, I asked him, "Are you still feeding those silly little animals?"

Sweating heavily, diving in and out of a burlap bag half filled with bran, he growled, "Not for long, brother-in-law. I'm getting rid of the friggin' things any day now. Hey, why don't you get us a couple of cold ones out of the ice box, Oberstdorf?"

Getting two quarts of beer from the kitchen refrigerator, I returned to the basement where Eppie was sitting on the feed sack, looking unhappy, while his livestock scurried and squealed in their cages. After a long pull at his bottle, my brother-in-law took a soiled towel out of a box, and began to wipe the dampness off his gaunt body.

"I got me a good deal," he announced between swigs at the bottle. "I'm trading my hogs for six acres."

Knowing him, I was skeptical. "Where are the six acres?"

"Right at the junction of 87 and 72."

"Hey, you're kidding!"

"Nope. Cross my heart and hope to die, Obie."

"Let me get this straight, Epworth Jarl. You have made a deal to trade a couple of hundred little furry animals for six acres of land at the fork of Highways 87 and 72—right here in Neu Koblenz."

"Well, yes—more or less."

"What does that mean—more or less?"

"Naturally, I have to give a little to boot," he admitted.

"How much?"

"Oh, about three grand."

"*About* three grand?"

"Three thousand, two hundred and twenty-six dollars, Obie. Damn, but it is hot down here!"

"Eppie," I said, "the older you get, the *crazier* you get. What in the world are you going to do with six acres of land between two highways at the edge of town? That is a motel site, or a truck stop location. Where do you plan to get that kind of money?"

"I don't need a lot for what I have in mind, Felix.

Come on upstairs and have a look at my architectural drawing.''

He had it on the wall of his bedroom, three feet by four, in India ink, with the architect's Spencerian signature in the lower right hand corner. At the top of the drawing, in shaded, block letters, I read "Jarl's Pioneer Land," and the drawing was of a frontier fort, complete with corral, barracks, trading post, sod house and Indian tepees.

"Look at that," my brother-in-law crowed. "I charge two dollars for adults and fifty cents for kids under twelve, just to go inside the fort and look around. Babies in their mothers' arms are free.''

"What's inside the fort that is worth two dollars?''

"Oh, the usual stuff that you see—a Gatling gun or two, period furniture in the sod house, real live Indians around the tepees. Get this, Felix—I'm going to have horses and cows in the corral. A lot of kids from back east have never seen horses and cows—or least not up close. Look at all the summer tourists coming from the east and the south, going to the Blue Hills and the Rockies! Man, this is the beginning of the west, Oberstdorf!''

"It sure is," I replied, dumbfounded that anybody could be so naive. "Where did you get the money to buy the land?''

"I'm borrowing on the house. It's paid for.''

"Where are you going to get the money to build the fort and buy the livestock?''

"I have that all figured out," he replied. "I don't really need six acres. Five will do.''

"So?''

"So I'll raffle off one acre. At a buck a chance, I can pay off the bank loan, then make a bigger loan to build the fort and buy stuff for the display. The sod house won't cost anything, Obie. I'll just strip enough sod off the six acres to build the house. Then of course, there will be a concession stand outside the entrance to the fort, where you can buy all kinds of Indian relics and mementos of the frontier."

"All made in Japan, I suppose."

"Not necessarily. You can get a nice line of authentic western memorabilia from Taiwan. Would you like to see my catalog?"

"I'd be delighted," I said, "some other time."

He was not done yet. "I plan to have a bunch of good-looking high-school girls all dolled up like frontier women and Indian maidens, to guide the tourists around the place, and to sell the souvenirs—"

I interrupted him. "Just a minute, P.T. Barnum. I am thinking about that six acres. Isn't that the big ravine where the river once ran—before it changed course in 1897?"

"What about it?" he demanded, lifting his bottle high to drain it."

"What *about* it? How are you going to level that big ditch?"

He was unshaken. "Easy, just fill it with dirt."

"*What* dirt?"

"I haven't figured that out yet," he admitted, "but I will."

Shaking my head in awe, I went into the living room and flopped down on a Naugahyde sofa and finished my beer while staring at Eppie, trying to think of something more to say. He got another two quarts of beer out of his icebox, as he likes to call it, and we relaxed on the sofa, looking at each other warily. The guy was beginning to overwhelm me with his goofy ideas, although I should have been used to it after twenty-three years. He's always been that way, but it's been worse since the kids left home. His son, Jon, is in the navy, and his daughter, Elsie, is married to a truck driver and lives in Hanover. With their departure, Eppie has had a lot of time to sit around alone and cook up cockamamie business schemes to make himself rich.

It's that way with many people. While the kids are at home, growing up, they keep you busy. If they are not sick or sniffling, they are getting ready for summer camp, or going out on dates, and you are sitting up half the night worrying about them. There are school plays, band concerts, family picnics and weekend fishing trips. You go through the agonies and ecstasies of little league baseball, high-school football, drivers' licenses, jalopies and senior proms. Then one day fatherhood is over, and you have time to sit around and ponder harebrained ideas for getting rich.

Of course, as I indicated earlier, Epworth Jarl has been a ding-a-ling as long as I've known him—a charming, likable, hard-working ding-a-ling, a certified weirdo. Had he put as much time and thought into his little produce business on Rhineland Avenue as he put into his goofy gimmicks, he'd be a rich man today. But he has a habit of leaping before looking. As an example—in 1973, he lost four thousand dollars promoting a rodeo in Blue Springs, primarily because the Shrine circus was playing in Neu at the same time and every Shriner in three counties was selling tickets to the circus. By the time Eppie's first cowboy came out of the chute on a bucker, there was not an entertainment dollar left

in the entire region. With his usual naiveté, old
Eppie blamed it on poor weather, bad luck, and
Lent. Anybody with a dime's worth of business
acumen would have seen what was going to happen. Jarl has been through all the standard con
games known to pulp magazine advertising—"we
need your song lyrics"—"our ghostwriter will
revise your book"—"raise squabs for pleasure and
profit," ad infinitum. He once owned eighty shares
of Northern Brewing Company Incorporated, which
was in business nearly six months, and he wasted
an entire summer in 1975 digging for jade on the
high mesa. You name a silly, stupid venture promot-
ed anywhere in Deerhorn County since 1953, and
my brother-in-law, Epworth T. Jarl, has been in on
it to some degree. If it were not for Arlene, Eppie
might be a skid-row bum, because in terms of business, he hasn't got the sense God gave little green
apples. Maybe that's why I like him so much—he
reminds me of myself.

Our wives came in, laughing and cackling the way
they do when they are together, dropped their bundles onto the dining-room table, and went into the
can together, causing Eppie to give me a funny
look. When they came out, they said hello, or something like hello, and went into the kitchen where
they started banging pots and pans around.

"Listen to all that pot banging," my host said,
looking at me glumly. "It's all a big act to give us
the impression that they are putting a big meal
together. What they are really doing is taking pots
and pans out of the oven so they can bake a frozen
pizza. Listen, Felix! Before long, you'll hear the
oven pop on and you'll hear the door open, and
then we'll have our tasty, fresh-baked pizza, with
cheese and pepperoni."

Eppie hates pizza, but has to eat it twice a week as the price of having a working wife. Because she helps out in the produce house, she is too tired to cook every night, so old Ep gets to eat a lot of fresh-baked frozen pizza, TV dinners and canned stew.

That day, however, she fooled him. She wasn't baking pizza but runzas, which were not available at the store. She had started from scratch with the runzas, which are basically little loaves of bread filled with hamburger, cabbage and onions. You can vary the filling, if you wish, using cheese, kraut or green peppers.

Arlene had the dough rising and the filling cooked, waiting to be baked. She rolled kraut and meat into the dough while the oven was heating, and placed them on a baking sheet. When the oven got up to three-hundred-and-fifty degrees, she put the runzas in along with an apple pie that was ready to be baked. When that was done, my sister-in-law, a congenial hostess, called out, "Do you guys want another beer?"

We did, and she brought them in, a bottle in each hand, her oval face sweating. "I heard on the radio that you are having a big anti-crime rally in Hessberg tonight, Obie."

"Yeah."

"What's that?" Eppie demanded, reaching for the beer. "*What* kind of rally?"

So I told him about it, while he listened avidly, leaning forward from the hips. As I narrated, Arlene went into the kitchen, but returned shortly to suggest that her husband take a bath and change his clothes because he smelled like Guinea pigs.

"I'll be glad when you get rid of those darned animals," she complained. "You are getting so that you smell just like them."

"I'll take a shower," he promised, "before we eat. Who do you think did it, Felix? Who put out the contract on Barney and hired the torch?"

"Man, you know all the terminology, don't you?" I said, feigning admiration.

"I read a lot," he replied, "when I am not building business empires."

We both laughed at that, and I told him that I was pretty sure who the culprits were and that I meant to name them at the meeting that night.

"I'd sure like to be there, Felix. Is it open to the public?"

"Sure. Do you want to go? You can come over to our place for supper, and go to the meeting with me."

"What are *we* going to do?" Ellen demanded, coming out of the kitchen with a platter full of hot runzas. She put them on a hot pad in the center of the dining-room table, and picked up the packages, to carry them to a bedroom.

"Who is *we*," I asked, "you and your fleas?"

"My sister and me," she answered. "What are we supposed to be doing while you two are over at the town-hall meeting, minding somebody else's business?"

"You and Arlene are free to go with us," I told my wife. "It might do you some good to take part in a public forum."

The look she gave me said it all—Do me some good? You sound silly. What possible good would there be in my sitting in that drafty old hall, listening to a bunch of malcontents air their grievances about what is wrong with the town?

"Hah," she grunted, "you must have rocks in your head!"

"That goes for me, too," Arlene told us, bringing the apple pie in.

While Eppie was showering and changing clothes, I went out to the kitchen, where the coffee was percolating. When it was ready, I filled four cups and took them into the dining room.

While we were eating, the sisters were gossiping about some of their former classmates at Neu Koblenz High School.

"I guess Phoebe Filkins's daughter flunked out of college," Arlene told Ellen. "We always thought she was such a smart girl."

My wife scoffed. "*Smart*? Do you remember her aunt, Ida Wiese, spent most of her life in the booby hatch."

Arlene way puzzled. "Whose aunt?"

"Phoebe's aunt. She was Ida Jones before she married Jake Wiese."

"Oh," Arlene said, "that Ida. I guess her son and his wife never did get along. He was supposed to have had something to do with that Paulsen girl."

"Which Paulsen girl? Not that silly one who giggled all the time!"

"Yeah," Arlene told Ellen, and she pursed her lips in disgust.

Eppie favored me with a helpless glance, and I nodded agreement, but we didn't say anything. When we had had all the runzas we wanted, and a piece of pie and some more coffee, I suggested that we go take a look at his six acres, and he needed no urging. Getting into his pickup, we drove east to the place where 87 and 72 meet briefly, before going their separate ways once more. From the junction, 87 bores straight east, while 72 angles northwest, across the Indian reservation. Eppie's land was

right between the two roads, lying in a rough tri-
angle that straddled an ancient riverbed which was
once a channel of the wandering Deerhorn River.
Over a period of years, it had been honored as a
dump site by the citizenry of the town, and was
half-filled with trash. As we watched, ugly gray
rats scurried in and out of rusty cans and battered
car bodies, dragging their naked tails, wriggling
whiskered noses in search of food. In the bottom of
the ditch, pools of scummy water had gathered as
an aftermath of the storm, and pussy willows grew
out of the morass, waving fuzzy arms idly in the
breeze.

"I just got me a brainstorm!" Eppie cried excitedly.

"Oh, no," I said, "not another brainstorm!"

"This time it can't miss," he stated, at the same
time throwing an empty bottle at a running rat.
"I'm going to establish a sanitary landfill site,
Felix."

"Yeah? What is that?"

"*That* is new terminology," he advised me.

"What does it mean?"

"It means *dump*, and that is what I aim to do,
Brother Oberstdorf. I'll get me a dump truck and a
driver. Then I charge anybody that wants to dump
stuff a dollar a load. My driver, who will have to be
some retired man, will sit at the dump site and col-
lect the money. Then, at three o'clock every afternoon, he'll put up a No-Dumping sign, and go get a
few loads of sand to cover the trash. In about six
months, the hole will be filled with junk and sand.
Then, I'll spread a couple of feet of dirt on top, and
start building my fort." His eyes danced in excitement.

"Eppie," I said, "is it all right if I ask you a personal question?"

"Shoot," he replied, pushing out his chest.

"Well, Mr. Jarl, you are such a doggone genius. How does it happen that you haven't got two dimes to rub together? Here you are, fifty years old and broke. Did it ever occur to you that maybe you haven't got what it takes?"

"I don't know," he answered. "I've never thought much about it, one way or the other. Listen, Felix, let's drive over to the Stockpen Bar and get us something to drink." Getting into his little truck, he ground on the starter until his motor caught, then shifted into low gear and pulled away, toward downtown Neu Koblenz.

Sitting beside him, I looked north to a long line of sandstone cliffs that shone golden red under a bright sun, then swung my gaze south to the blue ribbon of water that was the Deerhorn River, twisting its way through a narrow forest of bare trees, and all of a sudden, smelling the clean atmosphere of the day, I felt that tomorrow was going to be a new experience for me.

## 11

IT SEEMED LIKE A LONG WAY home, down the flat valley of the Deerhorn, facing into a red sun that was sinking into darkness on the western rim of the world. It had been a long, hard week, and I was weary. A stiff north wind was pushing at the car, making it a chore to stay on my own side of the white line, adding to my fatigue. My wife sat huddled in her corner, holding her otter fur collar up around her ears.

"I'm staying home tonight," she stated. "The windchill index is supposed to be minus twenty-three."

"We can drive to the town hall."

"Good," she said, "you drive and I'll stay home by the fire."

"You want to stop in Hanover for something hot—coffee or hot chocolate?"

"No, get me home before I freeze to death!"

We slowed down, but didn't stop, in Hanover, the halfway point from Neu. My gas gauge showed a quarter tank, and I like to have plenty of gasoline in my car at all times when the weather is cold, but I don't have the patience to stop for gas every time I should. So I didn't. It was only another twelve or thirteen miles to Hessberg, and a quarter of a tank was about five gallons. Nothing to worry about.

Sweeping in a great arc toward Mormon Crossing, we faced directly north into the bitter wind that shrilled past our windows. As it was now dark, my lights, which had been on for ten minutes, lighted up the highway ahead as we rushed toward home.

Leaning forward, Ellen reached out with her left hand to turn on the radio and get the six o'clock news. She wouldn't miss the six o'clock news for ten thousand dollars. My wife could be in hell with her back broken in ten places, and she'd dig up a radio and listen to the six o'clock news.

Just teasing, I asked her, "Would you like to stop in the Crossing for a hot drink or something?"

"No. I want to hear the news."

"Hell, you heard the news three times today. Things don't change that fast, Miss Schmidt."

"Quit bugging me." She was on the verge of a snit.

Skirting the settlement of Mormon Crossing, I caught the flash of fire from a hay-drying plant, and smelled the strong tea odor of quick-dried alfalfa hay. Rolling along at fifty-five, we pulled abreast a long freight train that was struggling to get up the grade going north. You don't notice the grade so much in an auto, which has two hunded horses to push a ton of weight, but a diesel engine pulling a hundred freight cars knows how much work it is. Most trains pick up an extra engine at the Crossing to help them over the rise, but even then it's not easy. The train moans and groans, swaying on the twin rails. It rumbles and roars as the great drive wheels of two powerful engines drag it up the six-mile grade. And approaching crossings, the lead engine lets out a wail that can be heard for miles up and down the valley.

Gaining steadily on the snaking freight, we finally moved ahead of it, grinding out the last seven miles and pulling into our home base at 6:24, leaving me plenty of time for a cup of hot jasmine tea before going to the meeting. While I was sipping my tea, the Jarls drove in. They had left Neu with us, but had taken the longer route, over hill and dale.

Coming into the kitchen with a small suitcase in one hand, Eppie cried, "Bbbrrr, it's colder than a loan shark's heart, Mr. Oberstdorf!"

"So true, Mr. Jarl. Do you want a cup of hot tea?"

"Okay, it smells real good. What is it?"

"Jasmine," I replied, and poured scalding water over a teabag that was waiting in a mug.

"Why don't you garage your car, Obie, and ride to the meeting with me?"

Before you get the idea that old Eppie likes to do favors by driving his car, let me set you straight. He is afraid to ride with anybody. He has this psychosis where he'd rather walk ten miles than ride in a car that somebody else is driving.

Having a little fun with him, I said, "Oh, that's all right, I'll drive. You can save your car for the trip tomorrow."

"I'll drive," he said firmly. "My car has not been driven enough lately."

His wife, who had come into the kitchen with my wife, reminded him that he had been to Win City the day before, a round trip of two hundred miles, and he gave her a dirty look. In return she smiled and picked up the bag that he had left on the kitchen floor.

"Take Heinie's room," her sister told her. "It's all made up." And while Arlene was taking the suitcase upstairs, Ellen put a pan of milk on the stove to heat for hot chocolate.

Stirring sugar into his tea, Eppie growled, "A couple of wise guys. I miss my Guinea pigs more all the time." Hunching over the table, he sipped his tea silently, reminding me of a stork all dressed up in an Eskimo suit. When the cup was empty, he stood up, pulled the hood of his parka around his head, and said, "Okay, Oberstdorf, let's get to the damn vigilante meeting."

Needless to say, my brother-in-law drove his car the nine blocks to our town hall, which, like most of our civic center, is elderly and weary. It is a redbrick structure built on two levels, the bottom level being a sub-basement, with the floor of the second level being six feet above the ground. The lower level has office space, a two-cell jail, toilets and a furnace room. Popeye Zorn, the combination night marshal, janitor and building manager, has an office in the first level. There is a daybed and a hot plate in his office, and he spends more time there than he does in his shack at the edge of town. The upper level is primarily a meeting hall, with a small stage at one end and a closed room at the other end. We store our folding chairs, tables and miscellaneous items in the closed room. For parties and weddings, Popeye puts a table across the open doorway and uses it for a lunch counter and bar.

In the old days, our town hall was the only meeting place in town for groups of more than a dozen people. Then, in 1898, we built a new courthouse, and two years later, the Turners built a clubhouse and gymnasium on the creek. The legion hall was built in 1947, and our new high school in 1958. So there are several meeting places now, but we still use the old town hall quite a bit, because it belongs to all of us, and because it is cheap and convenient. The rent is free, and all anybody who wants to use it has to do is contact Popeye a couple of days in advance to reserve it.

When we arrived, it was straight-up seven o'clock, and Irv Glotz was setting up seats, grumbling about it, because he would much rather have been home watching the bowl game on television. Eppie and I pitched in to help carry chairs out of the closet and set them up in rows before the apron of the stage, that was screened from the hall by a huge drop curtain painted all over with advertising of local firms, some of them long gone.

"You boys want to pull that curtain up?" Glotz asked, pleading with his gray-bearded, taciturn face. "My doggone back has been giving me hell lately."

"You know my brother-in-law, Epworth Jarl, don't you Irv?" I asked, going up a short flight of stairs at one end of the stage.

"I met him lots of times, back in the fifties when I was managing the town ball team. He used to play third base for Hanover. We beat them three years in a row for the league title."

"Sure you did," Eppie grinned, "using semipro pitchers from Win City."

Onstage I found some dangling ropes, and after a few experimental tugs, got the right one and hauled the curtain up exposing a bare floor that needed sweeping. While I was sweeping, citizens began drifting in, and Val Von Damm and Aubry Cozairt carried a long table and eight chairs out of the storeroom and set them up on the stage. Before long we had thirty people in the place, and it was only seven-thirty. But unless I missed my guess, there wouldn't be many more. It was a very cold night, and there was a football game on TV. Aside from that, meetings, however vital to the community or to an organization, don't usually draw huge crowds. Whether it is the legion, the Turners, V.F.W. or Chamber of Commerce meetings, you see the same faces, week after week, month after month. Some members are compelled by duty to attend meetings, feeling that it is a moral requirement of membership. Other men and women, for whatever reason, have nothing better to do. These are the perennial chairmen, recording secretaries, chaplains, sergeants-at-arms, vice-commanders, commanders, past commanders and adjutants. They trade offices from year to year, in a game of musical chairs reminiscent of that played with cabinet officers in the federal government. Some of these folks must honestly believe that without them, their clubs and guilds would simply fall apart. Yet others may enjoy some excuse, any excuse, to get out of the house for an evening. Then there are the status seekers who find their glory in club work. A person who is nothing in his own home or on his job may become the Lord High Poobah of Chapter 1604 after faithfully attending meetings each month for several years. This entitles him to wear the weird hat with the silver and gold stars pinned to it to denote his high rank. While in the club rooms, he is kowtowed to and exalted by chain-store managers, filling-station owners and insurance brokers, who normally hold him in contempt. Thus, it was no surprise to me that fewer than forty brave souls eventually showed up for our town meeting. They, in microcosm, represented all those referred to in the preceding paragraph.

Kurt and Leonard didn't waste any time in getting seats at the table, and were soon joined by Sam McKee and Horace Mann Himberger, looking like a cross between Buffalo Bill Cody and Mark Twain in his broad-brimmed hat, sack suit and string tie. He has a drooping, Twain mustache and a carefully brushed Buffalo Bill goatee. I doubt, however, that he can ride and shoot like Cody, and I know that he doesn't write like Mark Twain.

While these officials were settling around the table, as was their God-given right, cackling and preening like a bunch of Rhode Island Reds at a hen party, Abner Collins came walking in with a florid young man in civvies. Ab, who was in full uniform, introduced his companion as Lieutenant Francis Stakowitz of the state police, division of criminal investigation, and we began discussing the case in low tones. After a couple of minutes of non sequiturs, they sat down in the front row to continue their own critique.

A voice at my ear startled me. "Good evening, Mr. Oberstdorf," and when I looked around, it was the G-man, Jim Hawkins.

"Oh, hello," I replied, surprised to see him. "I thought that you were probably on your way to Washington, D.C., the land of the free and the home of the brave."

He laughed. "Hardly that, when my office is in Omaha. I decided to stay over and take in the meeting. It seems appropriate."

"Maybe more than you know," I told him. Then I introduced him to Collins and Stakowitz, and while

I was doing that, glanced toward the back of the room, where Junior Wagmann and Jack Braunholz were sitting together. They were both with a gray-haired chap in a tan Stetson and leather jacket. It was Dieter Emhoff, the cattle feeder, who has an ulcer and drinks Scotch whiskey in milk or cream. Between the trio and me were the Heffner-Borchers family, with Emmaline and Richard Porter sitting beside them, ill at ease in their Sunday best. The Porters are a childless couple who make all the meetings and never say anything. For them it's just a night out, away from the loneliness of their big house.

"Well," Kurt boomed amiably, having elected himself to chair the meeting, "shall we get started? I suppose you folks would like to get this over with and go home to watch the football game." He smiled idiotically, secure in his own humor. Nobody else seemed to be amused, and he went on. "Seriously, folks, a lot of us are alarmed at what has been going on in this county lately—murder, arson—God knows what else!"

"Bravo!" Snooks Hunter called from front row, left. "Amen!"

"Down with arson and murder," cried Virgil Warneke, one of our dozen town drunks, already nursing a snootful. "Up with clean living!"

Rising from his chair, putting the big hat out onto the table, Horace Mann cleared his throat pompously, and held up a veined hand for silence. "This is no laughing matter, Mr. Warneke. Your local press takes a very dim view of the scandalous events of the past two weeks. If we are not to succumb to complete anarchy, we must return to some semblance of law and order."

Virgil favored the editor with a dirty look, but did not attempt to defend himself. Then, Popeye Zorn came in to whisper something in Irv Glotz's ear. Appearing to be startled, the marshal got up and followed his deputy out into the night. As if by prearrangement, three of the four members of our esteemed city council, along with the city clerk, Freddy Ellender, came in and went up on the stage.

"Where did Irv go?" Hohenstein demanded, looking out at us for an answer. "Don't tell me that there has been another murder or fire!" He looked really upset.

"Yes, there has," Warneke yelled. "I seen it on my way over here—at Loseke's Standard Station—in the toilet!"

"What happened?" O'Shay cried, leaping to his feet.

Slumping forward in his chair drunkenly, Virgil did not respond at once, and shaking him savagely with a hand like a slab of bacon, Von Damm demanded, "Who got killed, Virgil? What happened at the station?"

Jerking himself erect, Warneke hiccuped, then said, "Read all about it in the *Hessberg Hesperus*. I seen the whole thing, and I'm selling exclusive rights to the local paper."

"Tell us what happened," Von Damm cried, "before I break your Goddamned neck, you drunken bastard!"

"It was terrible," Virgil said, covering his eyes as if to close out the horror of it. "A big, hairy cockroach choked a little bedbug to death." He began to laugh, shaking in glee.

"When the marshal gets back," Leonard said

angrily, "I'm going to have you locked up as a public nuisance!"

Virgil sneered. "The same to you, Cocky! Why don't you quit harassing law-abiding citizens and go out after that killer?"

"What's going on in this town?" asked Art Braun, one of our councilmen. "Dead bodies seem to be turning up all over the damn place!" He looked at O'Shay, who replied unctuously that the deaths might have been nothing more than a series of unfortunate accidents.

That brought Frankie Heffner steaming out of his seat, to lash out angrily, "My dad didn't kill himself! It was murder, Mr. O'Shay!"

The kid's mother tried to settle him down. She patted his shoulder, and spoke to him softly, but he didn't cool off right away. He sat fuming silently as the county attorney addressed him, "I appreciate your hurt and anger, young man, but there just isn't any proof of murder. Wouldn't you say that, Mr. Hohenstein?"

He looked for affirmation to Kurt, who nodded in agreement, saying, "That's about it, Mr. O'Shay—no hard proof."

Noting that there were women in the hall, Kurt, flashing his patented, vote-getting smile, said, "We seem to have a distinguished member of the state police here tonight. Do you have anything to add, Mr. Stakowitz? Pardon me—*Lieutenant* Stakowitz."

Getting heavily to his feet, Stakowitz turned to face the rear. "Thank you, Sheriff. No, there is not much to add, except that we have been looking into the matter and feel that there is enough circumstantial evidence to justify a complete investigation into the possibility of murder. As you ladies and gentlemen may know, the man burned to death in the elevator fire was wearing asbestos gloves. That pretty well established him as an arsonist, and it enabled us to identify him by taking his finger-prints. The man was a professional criminal, not just some transient looking for a warm place to sleep.''

Caught by surprise, the sheriff was speechless for long seconds, before managing, ''Well, of course, if you have new evidence—''

''No new evidence, Mr. Hohenstein. Pardon me, *Sheriff*. It is routine stuff, dug up by Mr. Oberst-dorf. All we did was verify it. We *did* this day inter-view a certain witness, and we'll be conducting an official investigation beginning Monday.''

It was all new to me, because up to that point, I didn't think that *anybody* was backing me, except the kid. The lieutenant's reference to a witness probably meant Charlie Wolf, who might have been a witness to monkey business, but certainly not to murder or arson.

Standing up, signaling Kurt and Lenny to be quiet, Sam called for me to come up to the platform, and when I obliged, said, ''Would you be kind enough to bring us up to date, Mr. Oberstdorf?''

That seemed to take the wind out of the sails of O'Shay and Hohenstein, who sat pouting and ex-changing glances while I began to deliver my theory. ''Ladies and gentlemen. In the past two weeks, I have spent a great deal of time on the in-vestigation of this case, and have arrived at some conclusions. To begin with, I should specify that I knew Barney Heffner very well, and am convinced that he could not have killed himself accidentally.

Having hunted with him many times over a period of years, I know that hunting safety was a religion with him. Under no circumstances would he shoot himself while crawling through a fence—especially when there was an unlocked gate thirty feet away." Pausing to let that sink in for a few seconds, I continued. "Barney's little dog—his constant companion—was found nearby, shot to death by a small-bore weapon, probably a twenty-two caliber. We know that Barney did not kill his own dog, because for one thing, he did not have any weapon with him when he was found but his shotgun. What reason would he have for killing his dog, then throwing the weapon away or hiding it? For that matter, he would not have killed the dog, anyway. He loved the little devil. No, somebody murdered the dog, then his master, probably with the same twenty-two caliber weapon. After that, the killer shot Barney with his own shotgun to mask the evidence of murder and make it look like an accident."

While I spoke, people were moving up from scattered seats in the hall, getting closer to me all the time, listening hard. A few came right up to the apron of the stage, to stand watching me. I told them about the mysterious rifleman who had fired at me in the park, about Thad Miller and the license number, and finally all about my part in the auto accident of Brian Keelan.

"Now," I said, "I am going to tell you my theory about who hired the two convicts, and why."

"You better have some proof," Lenny warned me, "before you start throwing accusations around!"

"Yeah," Kurt said, scowling at me.

Irv and Popeye came into the hall, and with them

a wave of arctic air that brought a collective shiver
to the gathering.

"All right," I said, "you all know that Barney was
an honest, independent man, and that he was curious and bright."

There was a murmur of approval from the audi-
ence.

"He did a lot of work hauling grain and livestock,
mostly grain." Spotting Milly, I saw that she was
dabbing at her eyes with a dainty, embroidered
hanky. I went on. "Just suppose that in the course
of his work, Barney came across some kind of un-
ethical, even illegal activity. Say that he learned
about a theft of grain, for instance, from a big elevator full of government grain." Glancing to
Emhoff and Braunholz, I could sense that they
were squirming. "To simplify it," I continued,
"let's assume that the grain was being hauled out
and fed to livestock, and that the grain dealer and
the livestock feeder were in cahoots." Faces began
to turn toward the back of the room, to stare at the
two affluent citizens. "Let's suppose some more," I
said. "Let's suppose that the partners, having
learned that Barney is onto them, decide to scare
him into silence. They go down to the city and hire
a paroled convict to come up here and put the bit on
Barney. He watches the Heffner house for a few
days, then follows Barney up to the mesa and
threatens him—only Barney does not scare easily.
He points his shotgun at the man, who empties his
automatic pistol into Barney, then shoots him with
the shotgun. He reloads, if he has to, and shoots the
dog and tosses him into the big ditch. Now the two
conspirators have nearly emptied an elevator of
two hundred and fifty thousand bushels of corn,

and are getting worried that a murder investigation
may discover the loss. They decide to hire an arsonist to burn the elevator, to destroy the evidence of
their theft. Unfortunately, they hire a friend of
Keelan's who is an auto thief, but not an arsonist.
He botches the job, and in doing so, gets himself
killed." Looking hard at Emhoff and Braunholz, I
told the citizens, "The conspirators will have to
face charges of grand larceny, conspiracy to arson,
and conspiracy to murder."

Dieter and Jack rose silently and left the building,
followed by forty-odd citizens bent on gossip. Within twenty-four hours, I knew, every man, woman
and child in Hessberg would learn about them.

Acting as if he were about to strangle, Lenny
O'Shay cried, "You've made some very serious
charges, Felix!"

Pretending to be surprised, I asked him, "*What*
charges? I didn't make any charges—just presented
a theory. There were some forty witnesses here.
They didn't hear me make any charges."

Coming up onto the stage like some great, blond
polar bear clambering onto an iceberg, Junior Wagmann told me, "Felix, I represent Braunholz and
Emhoff, and they have authorized me to file a suit
against you for defamation of character."

"*What* defamation? *What* character? I didn't
mention any names."

"You didn't have to. You made it clear enough."

"I'll make it a lot more clear," I advised him,
"when the case comes to trial."

"What case?" the county attorney demanded.
"You haven't *got* a case. Everything is circumstantial."

"Write this all down, Mr. Himberger," I said,

looking at the publisher. "It may come in handy the
next time we have an election. Be sure to get it
straight—County Attorney Denies Warrant in Heffner Case, also, Sheriff Refuses to Arrest Suspects in
Arson."

Momentarily bewildered, the old man began writing it down in his notebook.

"I didn't refuse anything," Kurt cried. "If O'Shay
wants to issue a warrant, I'll arrest both them high
and mighty dudes!"

"Get that down, Horace Mann—Sheriff Agrees To
Arrest the High and Mighty."

"Just a minute," Junior cut in. "You guys will
need more than that to go on."

"We *have* more," I told him. "For one thing,
there is a bartender in Win City who saw Keelan
with Emhoff."

Junior scoffed. "Is that all?"

"Not quite. Prison records show that the two
dead men, Keelan and Feenan, were cell mates in
the state pen."

"Anything else?"

"Yes. Charlie Wolf will spill his guts about what
Barney told him—if he hasn't already told the state
police. I believe that Charlie saw a lot while working in the feedlot. And on top of that, I assume that
the Department of Agriculture will have some
F.B.I. agents on the case. Is that correct, Mr. Hawkins?"

I looked at the G-man for confirmation, but he
wriggled out of it by saying, "No comment, Mr.
Oberstdorf."

"Well, I'll give you a comment," I told him. "As a
taxpayer, I want to see some justice done. You can't
let some yokel steal a half million dollars worth of

government corn and get away with it. I'll be on the telephone Monday morning, talking to both my senator and my congressman in Washington!"

Reluctantly, then, he admitted that the F.B.I. was already on the case. That seemed to impress the lawyers and the sheriff.

"I don't get it," Sam McKee said, screwing up his face in bewilderment. "These fellows are the two richest men in Kornfeld County—multimillionaires. Why would they steal corn like a couple of common thieves?"

"I see it all the time in my line of work," Kurt boasted. "It's just greed, Mayor. The more some people have, the more they want."

I had my own idea. "Maybe Braunholz got extended too far. He may be land poor. Possibly the chance to make a quarter of a mil in a hurry, tax-free, was more than he could resist. The bigger you get, sometimes, the freer you feel to make your own rules. Chances are that Jack began to think of the corn as his very own."

"What about Emhoff?" Art Braun asked. "How did he fit in?"

"Look," I replied, "anytime you can buy corn at a buck a bushel, on credit, you can make a lot of money. They couldn't just steal the corn and sell it on the open market, but they could feed it to steers, then sell the steers, without attracting a lot of notice. Chances are that Jack sold the grain to Dieter at a buck or a buck and a half a bushel—half the market price. So, they each made a quarter of a million dollars on the grain theft." Glancing at a subdued Friedrich Wagmann junior, I said, "By the way, counselor, tell your clients not to try anything with Kavich and Wolf, because the state police have them both under surveillance." That was not true to my knowledge. I made it up. "Also, you should know that in addition to everything else, Emhoff could be charged with bribery."

"Bribery!" the big one cried. "What are you talking about? Who did he bribe?"

"How about Charlie Wolf for starters? One day he is off work, asking for welfare so his family won't freeze and starve, the next day he is back on the Emhoff payroll, full-time, retroactive to the day he was laid off. Does that sound like bribery to you? Or did old Dieter suddenly buy himself a halo?"

Staring at O'Shay in resignation, Junior asked, "Can we get together on this Monday morning, early?"

Glancing at me, almost in request for my approval, the county attorney answered, "Okay. Bring your clients in at nine o'clock. I'll have my girl ready to take their statements."

Nudging me roughly, Eppie said, "Hey, Obie, we better get home, those Schmidt girls will have supper on the table. You told Ellen that we'd be back by nine."

"Let them wait," I said, flushed with victory. "I'm going to stop at Pete's for a drink."

As a kind of hint that we should be leaving, Irv and Popeye were folding chairs and carrying them to the closet, and I offered to help.

"While you are doing that," Jarl said, "I'll go downstairs and call in—tell the girls we'll be a little late."

Following my lead, the townsmen who were still in the hall began folding and carrying chairs, and before long, they were all put away, giving Irv a chance to get home for the second half of the football game. I forgot to ask him what he and Zorn had run out of the building for earlier, but it must have been some kind of false alarm, because I never did hear anything more about it.

Ep was waiting for me at the front door when I went down. "Your wife says that they had chili for supper and it is still on the stove. If we want some when we get home, we can heat it up. There are crackers and coffee cake in the cupboard."

He led me toward his car, and I asked, "Is that all?"

"No. She said not to wake her up when you get home."

"Oh."

By the time we got to Pete's, everybody in the place knew about the vigilante meeting, as it came to be called. People came to our booth in droves, asking questions, throwing out advice and opinions with wild abandon. Jay Clements, who just about lives in saloons, insisted upon buying a round. That entitled him to sit down with us and tell us all about Emhoff and Braunholz, both of whom he detested.

"We ought to string them lousy bastards up," he growled. "They'll get off scot-free. Mark my words, Obie, nobody with a lot of money ever gets sent up! But just let some poor fool with ten or twelve hungry kids get caught stealing a loaf of bread, and they throw away the key!"

My brother-in-law, glowing under the influence of his third boilermaker, had to agree. "That's right! I knew an old boy over at Neu who got three years for stealing a slab of bacon from a grocery store." He stared at me owlishly.

"See that," Jay yelled, glaring at me, "your own

Goddamned brother-in-law will tell you there ain't no justice!''

Eppie, who was watching the waitress, interrupted whatever pontification was coming next. "Wowee! Look at that Pocahontas! Would I like to have that movement in my watch!''

"She's half Indian and half Scotch," Jay told him. "Tight and wild. You can't hardly find that kind no more, Eppie.''

Squeezing out of the booth, I went to the bar and told old Pete to send us another round, then I put a coin into the juke to play three polkas, beginng with the "Liechtensteiner," my favorite, next to that classic, "The Beer Barrel Polka." When I returned to the booth, Eppie, who was involved with the waitress, tried to get me involved. "You want a hamburger, Obie? This cute little girl here tells me that they have great hamburgers.''

"No, thanks," I said. "Don't forget the chili, and the little girl at home." I winked at Jay, who didn't get it.

Slapping my leg playfully, Brother Jarl laughed and told the girl, "Bring me a cheeseburger with fries, miss. My father here does not want anything—to eat, that is." He laughed again, inanely, as he does when he is getting too much to drink.

Clements, having delivered his legal opinion, lurched to his feet and walked unsteadily toward another part of the room to find companionship. He was replaced by the waitress, Wilma Featherbow, who had taken Eppie's order to the cook and then brought our drinks from the bar. Taking two boilermakers from the tray, I asked her to deliver the other to Jay Clements, and I dropped a five onto the tray and told her to keep the change. If that sounds like overtipping in a neighborhood bar, it was not. The girl had brought three rounds to our booth without receiving a gratuity.

"Thank you very much," she said, and to Eppie: "Your cheeseburger will be ready in five minutes, sir."

As she walked away, he gave me a long look, saying, "*I'm* ready *now!*"

About that time, I began to be lionized anew as fresh squads of judges came into the place and spotted me. People swarmed around, wanting to talk, trying to buy me drinks, causing me to appreciate how David must have felt after disposing of Goliath. There is, of course, a tendency to hail the winner and impugn the loser, as evidenced by a gang of dogs in a fight. If you have ever witnessed this, you know that when one dog is down, his erstwhile friends will attack him viciously, to rip and tear at him, even kill him. Human animals are much the same, with the added incentive provided by their emotions and hates. They will bow and scrape to those in power, but turn upon them with bared fangs when they are down.

Ace Zeeb got my ear to tell me that he knew a lot about Emhoff and Braunholz and would go on the stand if I needed help. It was probably drunk talk, but I made a mental note of it, anyway. Sometimes it's difficult to separate fact from fantasy.

Dan Focek boasted that he could tie Braunholz in with Keelan—more drunk talk, no doubt, but again I made a mental note, at the same time wondering why these people had not come forward when I needed them, if they really knew something.

"Let me in here to see my cousin," Katie Mertz yelled, and the Red Sea of humanity parted before the onrush of my cousin's wife. "Come on, Obie, let's dance. I haven't seen you in a month of Sundays!" Hauling me out of the booth like a sack of feed, she dragged me to the postage-stamp dance floor and began to hop, skip and jump to the music—or almost to the music. As the red, blue and yellow lights of the box began to mingle on the floor to produce a spectrum of color, she started yacking at me about old times and family picnics. Katie, who is married to my second cousin, Manfred Mertz, is six feet one, and weighs two thirty-five naked. But don't get the idea that she is fat, because she isn't. She is just big. Her husband, Manny, is even bigger, and they have four boys, the smallest being about the size of a yearling rhinoceros. And their three girls are nearly as large.

"Give me a half dollar," she demanded. "I want to play the juke."

While she was punching the box to select her numbers, I slipped away back to the booth to take a drink out of my beer glass.

My brother-in-law was reciting the minutes of the vigilante meeting, giving me a lot of credit, of course. "You guys should have seen Obie—my brother-in-law, you know. He really put them shysters down! We married sisters—the famous Schmidt sisters of Neu Koblenz." Even in his cups, Epworth Jarl has a kind of humor. "Hey, there, Felix, these gentlemen want to buy us a drink."

As he was getting crocked, it was time for old Ep to be going home to Arlene. Otherwise, she would blame me for it, and there would be a family misunderstanding—mostly with my own wife, who is very protective of her little sister. But I left the barroom reluctantly, because it was my finest hour, and I hated to see it come to an end simply because I had to take a drunken man home to his Frau.

When Wilma Featherbow came over to get another order, I told her that we were leaving, and I pushed all the money on the table into a pile and scooped it onto her tray with one hand. Then I told her, "Listen to me, Wilma Featherbow, if you ever need any welfare or anything, come up to see me."

Gazing at me with her great, green gray eyes, the young woman nodded, but she was only kidding, or humoring a senior citizen, because several months have passed, and she has not been up to see me.

So the night of Goliath ended for me. The novelty of a fat little David, who confronted not one, but two Goliaths, wore off, leaving us alone in the booth. We drank up and went outside, into an icy wind that made us huddle in our parkas. After getting into Eppie's car we drove home, where we took off our shoes and jackets and sat in the living room with our wives, who were dozing through a 1937 horror film on television.

# Epilogue

WELL, THIS IS THE WRAP-UP, so to speak, of the
Heffner case, a resume to sort of tie up the loose
ends. O'Shay and Hohenstein were right all the time
about the circumstantial evidence. It was really all I
had, but as time passed things fell into place.
Braunholz went to trial first, and spent just about
every dime he could dig up. There was a big hulla-
baloo about a change of venue, and his lawyers,
Finke, Levinson, Caruso and Sullivan, of Win City,
managed to get the trial moved to Hanover on the
basis that old Jack would not get a fair hearing in
Hessberg. Braunholz had fired Wagmann in favor of
the slickers from the city, in their three-hundred-
dollar suits. There is an expression in the German
language that fits this situation to a tee—*fremd-
sucht*, meaning in broad translation, a love of strangers, an admiration for things that are foreign or
distant. This was the thing that led many Germans
to latinize their names in the Middle Ages. It is the
same thing that motivates some people to buy ex-
pensive French wines when New York or California
wines would taste better and cost less. There is not
a better, shrewder lawyer anyplace in the country
than Friedrich Wagmann Jr., who was hired by
Klaus Borchers to help O'Shay in the prosecution.
The county attorney made Junior his assistant, to

keep it legal, of course. By some coincidence, both prosecutors turned up with new Lincoln automobiles after the trial—Klaus Borchers is a silent partner in the Lincoln-Mercury agency in Blue Springs. Lenny and Junior tore into the city lawyers like a pair of well-trained police dogs—one a yappy terrier, the other a lumbering, sagacious Saint Bernard. Between them they made mincemeat of the defense, and one can guess that Braunholz was sorry he didn't keep Junior on retainer. If nothing else, it would have prevented his helping O'Shay in the prosecution. The trial dragged on for six weeks, with a long procession of witnesses that I had never heard of. They seemed to come out of the woodwork and out from under rocks. Eventually Jack was found guilty of grand larceny and conspiracy to arson. He got five years and five years, to run consecutively, so will have to serve at least six years in the pen, if he ever runs out of appeals. If he's lucky, he'll run out of appeals before Barney's relatives run out of patience. Frankie has not made any threats, but spends most of his weekends target shooting up on the mesa. He blames Braunholz as much as he blames Emhoff, although the feeder did not implicate Jack in the hiring of Keelan. There is a rumor that Klaus Borchers has contracts out on Emhoff and Braunholz, afraid that if they ever go to prison, they will get out early. This is probably pure scuttlebutt, having no basis in fact, but it has both men worried sick. Braunholz has lost thirty-five pounds, and his face is sagging like a line of wet laundry on wash day. Emhoff, who had less to lose than Jack had, is a living skeleton.

Emhoff employed another Win City law firm, Chlodek, Van Horne, Panduski and Chlodek, to defend him. His charges were receiving stolen property and conspiracy to commit murder. He was found guilty and received a total of twenty years at hard labor. He, too, has filed several appeals and may never serve a day, criminal justice being what it is. If he does go in, he'll never come out, because he is past sixty now and in very poor health.

Charles Wolf, who blew his guts to help convict Emhoff, lost his job at the feedlot, but got a better job driving a truck for Borchers. If one can judge by the way he furnished his house and dressed his family after the trial, old Klaus probably gave Charlie more than just a good job. In retrospect, about all he really did was talk about what Barney told him in reference to the grain going from the elevator to the feedlot. But it was one piece of evidence in the patchwork quilt that O'Shay and Wagmann stitched together in court.

In case you are interested, my boys did come home for Christmas, but Heinie did not date Sissy Borchers. Earl did, while Heinie spent most of his vacation studying and making long distance calls to Louisiana. We didn't know it until he came home, but he has been dating a girl from Baton Rouge. According to her picture, she is very pretty, and according to what Heinie says, her daddy is very wealthy. And that is a hard combination to beat.

Yes, Frankie and I did file claims on the coal vein, and I sold my share to Klaus for twenty-five thousand dollars, just to let them keep it in the family, and to provide myself with a little walking around money. Then I bought into Eppie's six acres, more or less as an act of charity. The landfill idea did not work out, and we don't know how we are going to get the hole filled up, but no doubt